At the
Threshold of
Love

At the Threshold of
Love

NAMITA SONTHALIA

Srishti
PUBLISHERS & DISTRIBUTORS

SRISHTI PUBLISHERS & DISTRIBUTORS
Registered Office: N-16, C.R. Park
New Delhi – 110 019
Corporate Office: 212A, Peacock Lane
Shahpur Jat, New Delhi – 110 049
editorial@srishtipublishers.com

First published by
Srishti Publishers & Distributors in 2017

10 9 8 7 6 5 4 3 2 1

This is a work of fiction. The characters, places, organisations and events described in this book are either a work of the author's imagination or have been used fictitiously. Any resemblance to people, living or dead, places, events, communities or organisations is purely coincidental.

The author asserts the moral right to be identified as the author of this work.

Dedicated to that one emotion
that keeps you going - LOVE!

Acknowledgments

"To love is nothing. To be loved is something. But to love and be loved, that's everything."

– T. Tolis

We seldom get an opportunity to thank those who make a difference in our lives. Here, I have the most beautiful way of expressing my gratitude towards those whose presence makes my world what it is.

What makes me what I am is God, and thus, I want to begin by saying that he is the force that makes me move forward in life. To help me idealize him in all his glory, he blessed me with a family and set of friends who fill me up with life.

I dedicate my book and all of myself to my mother, Mrs Madhu Bajaj, for as the song goes – "all of she, loves all of me"!

To my dad, Mr Naresh Bajaj, for being the hand that held me when the tides were rough and the arms that enveloped me when I needed a safe haven.

To my in-laws – Dad, Mr Pradip Sonthalia and Mom, Mrs Kiran Sonthalia – for showing me what unconditional love is all about, standing by as my pillar of strength, having faith in me.

To my husband, Ankit Sonthalia, for being the critic who made me who I am, standing by my side through it all.

To my brothers and sister, Aditya Vikram Bajaj, Anant Bajaj & Aditi Bajaj, for always being my strength, my confidantes and my laughter machines.

To Anshika and Kaashvi, for being my world.

To my best friends. You know you mean the world to me.

To Arup Bose and Stuti at Srishti Publishers, and their team, for being the reason why this book is no longer my imagination, but much more.

To *love* and everyone who personifies that emotion in my life.

To know more about me and my work, or to send in your suggestions and feedback, do write to me at namibajaj@gmail.com.

I have always believed in love. To be honest, I was certain it would hold the most valuable place in my life, my existence. And as a matter of fact, it did!

I have often heard that one does not always dream with their eyes closed. In fact, it is those dreams that one sees with their eyes open that meet their fulfilment.

In my case, this dream was 'love'.

And so, I lived in it, celebrating it in the lives of others. But when it came to love forming a part of my life – *that* was yet to happen!

I thought I was prepared. Like most of us, I thought I knew how I wanted my life to unfold. I had indeed conjured it all in my head. But then, it came without knocking at the door!

I am Ahaana Agarwal and I live in my own flamboyant little world. There is nothing pretentious about me, although people may say I am those 'no-nonsense' types. At twenty-six, five–feet-four, fair, dark brown hair and eyes that, according to people, could really look into your soul, my ways are as natural as any other girl walking past you. But with my hidden secret, desires and aspirations, I do feel special in one of god's own ways!

Done with my high school, I took up event management as my field of work. Making arrangements for marriages, baby showers, parties and shows became the centre of my life. It let me be a part of the happiness in everybody else's life.

I saw friends from college having crushes, and eventually getting married to the love of their lives. Witnessing the gleam in their eyes of living their dreams, I believed that there was someone who was living just for me... somewhere out there.

Like every young girl, I too blink my eyes fondly when I dream of my 'Mr Perfect' and playfully dedicate all the romantic songs I hear to that faceless man. Every time I host a wedding under my company banner – The Threshold of Love – I cannot help but sigh as I inhale the air intoxicated with the ardour of romance and devotion, hoping for it to come into my life as well.

But then, fancying the thought of how it appeared before me is something I call the hand of destiny.

How it all began...

It was one of those days when nothing would work according to plan! The drafts, props, music player, staff... it felt like today was the day when everything was meant to go wrong.

We had a three-year-old's birthday event coming up in three days and the props that we had ordered were either simply not in sight or plain wrong. My friend and business partner, Ansh, was too busy finding a bride, and thus was on his way to his date. *(Yet another arranged marriage. Oh! Never mind...we shall get back to him later.)*

And that left me with no help in foreseeing every arrangement. *The thought of handling it all alone got to me.*

I just picked up the phone and dialled Mishka's number, the only other person after Ansh, who really knew how a crisis situation affected me.

Speaking of Mishka, she is someone very sweet, totally filled with the right words for the right hour. Not too tall, about five-feet-two, with jet-black hair and glasses, her ways are subtle and friendly. Although she is a tad shy, no one is immune to her infectious smile.

Rolling out a little secret before you, the day she joined us, which was almost two years ago, it was almost written on her face that she had a huge crush on Ansh.

Thinking of *why that* happened, it doesn't surprise me at all. Ansh – who is quite tall at five-feet-eleven and well built, showing off his regular gym workouts – is always the charmer and yet the humble man. Poetic in nature and always ready to help, he is someone who is well aware of his good looks, but is modest enough to set his limits.

Thus, it was not so difficult for Mishka to be caught in a situation that people generally describe as 'love at first sight', when on her first day at office, she banged into him in the most fairy-tale manner while he was struggling to carry a huge bunch of files over to his desk.

"Yikes!" Okay, he did shout and all that, but cooled down on seeing the shy newcomer and displaying that easily forgivable side of him. And that smile – oh! That was all that was needed to sweep Mishka off her feet!

But the fact that today Ansh was out with his parents visiting a girl must have triggered things in Mishka's head, causing her to skip work.

"Hey Ahaana," said Mishka at the other end of the phone, making me snap back into reality as I stopped rocking my chair and got back to the problem at hand.

"Hi Mishka, how are you?" She was silent for a moment and it was so there – that 'he does not love me' sadness in her voice. I knew I had to give up on the idea of asking her to come and lend me a hand at work.

"Am okay," came a faint reply. "I am sorry for not turning up today, Ahaana. I know it must be a mess out there." And after a second's pause she said, "Okay, I am on my way to work."

"It's alright Mish, take the day off. I can handle it." With that, imagining a lame smile on her face, I hung up.

Now I only had me to take up on all that was 'not working out'. Sighing, I got back to work. I made calls, directing my colleagues to get all the decors in place and it went on from there.

Within a couple of hours, the balloons, outfits of cartoon characters, rhymes, tableware kits, banners and every other vital kids' accessory that we had planned for Manav Kalro's birthday party were put together before me for approval.

Too engrossed in my work, I did not notice him enter my office at first, and when I did, I could not take my eyes off him! A perfect face on a perfect body, he walked in with a stride that could almost make him pass for a Greek God.

A heart-shaped face, tanned complexion, almond like dark and deep-set eyes, all but highlighted his classy attire.

His dark wavy hair was dishevelled and as he walked in, he spread his hands across to smoothen them out. There was something about his gait that made me both nervous and anxious at the same time.

A small smile played at the corners of his curvy mouth and as he made his way towards me, he was all but making my heart melt that very instant.

I had never experienced such a weird frenzy in my head; this funny, flying kind of a feeling before. Numb at my toes, I sat still while I tried to glance away with all the reserve that I could manage. As he approached, the depressing thought that he might probably be here to get *his* marriage planned, dawned upon me.

While I was brooding, the handsome stranger was already at my desk, giving me a strange look. It was only then that I realised, I had been staring.

I guess my realisation was all too obvious because I noticed his smile get bigger. I glanced away and felt like cursing myself, for his smile told me that the colour must have reached my cheeks.

Obviously ignoring the effect he had upon me, he offered his hand for a handshake. "Hi, I am Ronit Malhotra."

His smile warmed up my entire office and then it suddenly reckoned to me that I was expected to reply.

"Hi! I... am... Ahaana Agarwal," I stammered, trying to gain composure. "What can I do for you, Mr Malhotra?" I glanced at him and then looked away as I awkwardly took his outstretched hand.

Now c'mon, he is probably a client. So get a grip. I scolded myself, as I mentally kicked my thoughts away. This was no time for a mindless resemblance to a sixteen-year-old with a crush.

"I am getting married this November..." and the rest of it was distant for a second, while I thought, so much for week knees and oh that boy...!

I cleared my head and tried to figure out what he must have said in the past few minutes. Holding onto my crippled confidence, I started with the practiced words and display.

"These are our most talked about outdoor weddings Mr Malhotra," I said, as I showed him the presentations of our various projects, professionalism taking over. We discussed the proposal for a while and though he looked serious, his face told me he had liked them.

He confirmed it by saying, "I am very happy to see that what I've heard about you guys is justified, Ahaana. I guess, this is it! My fiancé and I would love to have The Threshold of Love plan our wedding!" And so he went on, giving us the details that he wanted an outdoor wedding while I kept cursing myself for allowing my thoughts to wander.

"Staying in Bangalore, a perfect place with the perfect weather, it's usual that couples decide to have their weddings at resorts in and around the city. But the current trend of destination weddings is definitely trending," I tried to get on with business.

"It surely is and I would like just that!" He smiled softly.

It was decided that we would meet his fiancé and his family the coming week.

"So, I will meet you with my colleague at your place, sir."

"Sure, Miss Ahaana."

With that and a formal handshake, he walked out just the way he had come in.

Staring in the direction of his exit, long after he was gone, I tried to fathom the reason for the madness unfurling within me. 'This' was an unfamiliar territory that I had treaded onto and it had definitely given me shivers. Wiping off the sweat on my palm onto my denims *(was I that affected?),* I got back to my earlier and much safer project in hand – little Manav's birthday party.

In spite of having arranged almost fifty events so far, I still felt nervous at the beginning of every project, hoping for it to unfold with smiles and grandeur.

I reached the Kalro residence ahead of time. As I entered, they welcomed me with keen eyes while I prepared the games and other surprises for the kids. By three, the little invitees and their parents started to drop in. Every child received a fluorescent coloured wristband and radium sticks from Mishka, giving their excitement new bounds.

Once all the invitees had arrived, it was time for our team to begin the show. Joshi from our team was dressed up as Tom, the cat and another as Jerry, the mouse. As they entered, the kids shrieked with delight, making the Kalros and me giggle. The kids were taken into their favourite world of cartoons as Tom and Jerry played tricks on one another; especially making musical chairs a hit when the kids laughed hysterically as Tom chased Jerry and Jerry outran Tom!

The cake was in the shape of Superman. Manav, who was thrilled at seeing his hero on the cake, smiled in a manner that threw all my exhaustion outside the window.

Sighing, I sat back and relaxed as I felt proud of my job. With all the kids enjoying the games and dancing to the tunes of their favourite nursery rhymes and songs, it was yet another feather in our cap.

It was another of those regular days at my office. Mishka was at her desk, busy making drafts that were to be shown to our clients. The following weekend, Ansh and I had to meet the Malhotras at their residence, and a week later, begin with the wedding preparations.

It was noon when Ansh showed up at work almost after a week. Looking at his expressions, I knew his parent's sincere effort in searching for a bride for him had been futile.

"Hey Ahaana!" he said, trying to keep his tone normal. He came and sat at my table, a faint smile pasted on his face.

"Hi Ansh. Didn't work out, huh?"

He shook his head.

"You want to talk about it?" I went around pulling a chair next to him.

"I had to say no!" He looked so forlorn, I wished I could just crack him up with something more positive. But it was impossible to ignore the look on his face that showed the remorse he felt upon rejecting his parents' choice.

"I am not going to meet any girl unless I am sure that there could be something between us. It is not very pleasant to reject someone. But I am helpless, Ahaana. Why can't my parents understand that you cannot just meet someone and decide to spend your entire life together, unless of course it is love. Actually, you know what, the entire concept of an arranged marriage is faulty. I think a love marriage is more appropriate! At least, it does not cause such hurt of rejection to anyone." He was almost blabbering and all of it in one breath, making me smile.

"I understand Ansh!" I managed.

"No you don't. I think I don't want to marry anyone but for love," he countered as he exhaled.

He said this and I noticed Mishka, trying too hard to show that she was lost in work, trying harder to hide her delight that Ansh was still available. I hid my grin. At least Mishka had a chance.

"I think you are right!" I suppressed the urge to giggle as I saw Mishka's smile that almost split her face into two. "It must have been tough to reject someone. But it's all right, you know! After all, it's a matter of spending your life with the right person. Making a mistake there would be disastrous. So, cheer up!"

He simply nodded.

"Hey! Let's go get some lunch?" I suggested, trying to change the air that was heavy with dilemma, looking curiously at both of them.

"Sure. I do need some refreshing fun-time with my friends! Joining us, Mishka?" Ansh asked as he turned to look at Mishka, whose cheeks were matching crimson with her outfit.

"Yes, sh… sure," she said sheepishly.

"Great! Let's get going then," I said, smiling to myself as we headed out to one of the Chinese restaurants nearby.

"I have told Dad I will not be meeting any other girl!" Ansh began while we were waiting for our order to be served.

"I think that's a good idea." Mishka chimed in. Ansh and I smiled, although for different reasons.

"Well, I think I will not probe the marriage zone for another two years. Though the idea of being in love is quite intoxicating, my inner voice says otherwise," I said.

"What kind of a guy do you see yourself with Ahaana?" Mishka asked me.

Before I could reply, my childhood friend Ansh responded dramatically, "For her, the person will be a combination of every virtue man knows of, Mish. Someone tall, fair, handsome, kind and gentle. A man who will always stand by her side."

"That's every girl's dream man!" Mishka giggled, the light in her eyes betraying that she had not missed the endearment 'Mish' from Ansh.

"Oh, I heard we had a new client a couple of days back. So another wedding coming up, huh?" Ansh asked.

"Yep, it is going to be an outdoor wedding. They want to have it at a beach, so I think Goa would be the best place. What do you say?" I asked excitedly.

"Hey, now that's going to be a fun wedding," taking a deep breath, he added, "and with loads and loads of work!" He grinned back at me as I smiled. "So who is the client?" he asked.

"Ronit Malhotra and Taashi Gupta. Both are from Bangalore," Mishka informed him instantly.

"Nice! So when are we due for a meeting, Ahaana?"

"This weekend at the Malhotra residence. They have invited us for lunch. Mishka has already prepared the catalogue for the outdoor weddings. I think they would like an up-scale wedding with about just enough guests. And that we shall plan!"

Discussing the plans and various ideas, we enjoyed our steaming Chinese food and headed back to work.

After a satisfactory preparation had been done before our meeting with our prestigious client, I drove back home, tired and anxious for some quality time with my family and some good sleep.

Ours is a small family of four. Me being the older one, I have a little brother *(well, not so little now)*. His name is Krishna. Into his final year of engineering, he is totally pampered by all of us. Dad and I are usually out through the day; Krish remains either with his books or his friends and Mom with her boutique. It is only during dinner that we enjoy each other's company.

"I will be having an outdoor wedding this time Dad, and it's going to be in Goa in November!" I told everyone as we settled down for dinner.

"That is great, sweetheart! I am very proud of you and your team. In fact, I happened to meet Mr Kalro last week. He is a customer's friend, and he told me about the splendid job you did for their son's birthday party!" Dad said with a smile.

"Wow! Thank you Dad. That's a small world," I beamed.

"Goa is going to be beautiful in November. A nice time and place for a beach wedding," Mom exclaimed. "Is it a Christian wedding Ahaana?"

"No Maa. They are Hindus. Malhotras and Guptas."

"Oh! That is nice. Have you started with the preparations? There must be a lot of work. A wedding is the biggest event of one's life after all." My mother could be really dramatic when it comes to the things she wants to convey to us and right now, I know she was trying her best not to tread onto the topic of my marriage. Although, if she had her way, I would have been married for almost a good five years by now.

"Yes it is, Mom. We will be meeting our client this weekend. After that, the actual work will begin."

"Hey sis, can I join you this time? I will be finishing my exams now and will be free by November. I could also help you perhaps," Krish said.

"Sure Krish. You do deserve a break!" I told him fondly. Unlike other siblings, Krish and I rarely fought. Somehow, we both had found our best buddies in each other.

"I can design a beautiful lehenga for you Ahaana! You must look your best. Especially since it is an Indian wedding, people usually get very extravagant there. I want my daughter to outshine them all. Oh, and the list of suitors for you will become endless then!" My mother definitely couldn't control the urge, as I tried to ignore the comment. She was one of the top apparel designers in Bangalore, but at the end of the day, she was my mother who could not wait to get me married.

"I could use a good dress, Mom. I will let you know." I try to keep it as crisp as possible.

"You said it was Goa that your clients were thinking about, right? I could have a word with Mr Khaitan if you want any help with the bookings at any of the resorts." Dad, my forever saviour, came to the rescue.

"Sure Dad. That would be of great help. Just let us finalise the venue first." Mr Khaitan happened to be a man of means at Goa, someone my father knew well.

The rest of the dinner went by discussing our day and other big and small things. Life may be hectic with cut-throat competition, but the time spent with one's family provides the boost to face life with renewed energy. I smiled fondly at the three people whom I loved the most in this world.

We were to be at the Malhotras's residence by one in the afternoon. Ansh and I reached office by nine in the morning to discuss our plans. Mishka helped us chart down the best options and the themes that we hoped would be loved by Mr Ronit and his family. The wedding was due at the end of November, which gave us four-and-a-half months in hand to plan the event to its complete grandeur.

It was ten minutes to one when Ansh and I reached the Malhotra residence. Theirs was a beautiful white mansion with an elegant driveway. There was a huge fountain at the centre of a well-kept lawn. We noticed the affluent collection of expensive brands of automobiles in a row, making the driveway nothing less than a frame from a Bollywood movie. Ansh could not help his grin as he went on exuberantly flashing the names of the cars for my information. *It's a boy thing, I guess!*

Arriving at their porch, we were warmly received by Mr Ronit, accompanied by his mother Mrs Neeta Malhotra. The sight of him made my stomach curl. I decided to ignore it once and for all and directed my attention towards his mother, admiring her gait. She seemed like a lady of dignified beauty and composure. The excitement she portrayed was almost contagious.

Their house was lavish. We entered a huge living room that boasted of a marble clad wall with golden emboss at one end. It synchronized with the gold and copper decor of the rest of the living space elegantly. A small fireplace rendered a classy look to the rich and opulent decoration. Intriguing curios reflected sparingly across the structure, adding to the glamour. Huge windows opened to the garden outside, with sweet smelling flowers making the air resplendent with their aroma within.

A middle-aged man sat in the room with a wide grin pasted on his face. With a quick stride, he got up, approaching us with a manly gait. I was not wrong in guessing him to be Mr Malhotra, Sr.

He greeted us and introduced himself as Mr Deepak Malhotra. Shaking hands, we introduced ourselves and sat down for business. The happiness in the air was infectious, making us both smile back into those friendly eyes.

"I have heard a lot about The Threshold of Love," Mr Malhotra began while Mrs Malhotra beamed at us.

"All good things I hope," said Ansh, cheerfully.

"Oh yes, certainly! All lovely things which have made us decide upon you for my son's wedding."

"Thank you, sir. It is an honour," I chimed in.

"The honour is ours," he said smiling.

"We have created a portfolio that could help us begin with what you proposed to us, Mr Ronit," I continued.

"Yes, please. Let us see what you have!"

And we proceeded with our work, showing them the various proposals for decors and other requirements. We took notes of every suggestion and made a rough plan of action for a perfect wedding.

Soon, we were joined by Taashi Gupta, the bride to be and her family. As we were discussing, I noticed the impressive mannerisms of the two families. Taashi was a pretty, petite girl, but seemed quite indifferent to the arrangements being made for her wedding. Quite unlike Ronit, I found myself thinking. Pretty that she was, there was a touch of modesty that was missing there. *Anyway, marriages are made in heaven, or so I have heard!*

After having finally settled for Goa as the venue, we had to now zero down on the resort. We decided to leave for Goa in the first week of July for planning, and that meant fighting sunburn. It was decided that Ronit, Taashi and both their fathers would be travelling to Goa with us.

We still had a week's time in hand. I made good use of it in scheduling meetings with my contacts in Goa, earnestly hoping that the arrangements receive a positive response from the Malhotras and the Guptas.

It was Thursday afternoon and we had our flight the next evening. I was working on the Malhotra wedding project when the phone rang.

"Miss Ahaana? Hi!" said a familiar voice at the other end.

"Hello Mr Ronit. What can I do for you?" I replied, my forehead creasing involuntarily with a sense of worry.

"Well, I called because there is a small problem. Taashi and her parents have an urgent appointment this weekend and my father has to attend an important meeting on Saturday. Would it be a problem if we made the trip on Monday?"

Oh no, I thought! It was too late for postponing. I had already taken an appointment with Mr Khaitan. My Dad had arranged for a meeting with him this Saturday. *How would I deal with him? That man was definitely strict!* I knew I couldn't just say nothing and thus muttered what I had in mind.

"Umm... okay, Mr Ronit. I will see what I can do. It is just that I have had a meeting scheduled with one Mr Khaitan, who could really help us in arranging for the venue we had zeroed on. He is generally available on weekends and I had taken an appointment with him for Saturday afternoon."

He didn't say anything to that. Just a deep sigh. I hesitated for a second, and said, "Okay. Let me see what I can do. Perhaps I will leave on Friday as planned and the rest of you can come with Ansh?" After a hesitant pause, I pressed, "But the problem here would be that I would need you to see the resort that we will be booking for the wedding."

"I understand," he said. He was silent for a moment and that creepy sinking feeling returned in my gut. *What was it about this man that left me so unnerved even when he was miles away? Damn Ahaana,* I kicked myself mentally as I waited for his response.

"All right then, can we do this? I accompany you to Goa while Ansh brings my father, Taashi and her dad to the decided place? Will that be fine, Miss Ahaana?"

The thought of not having to deal with the wrath of Mr Khaitan delighted me. I cheerfully replied, "That would be just great. Thank you for understanding Mr Ronit."

"I think I can manage that. I am sorry about the sudden change though. I will be picking you up from your office at 6:30 p.m?" *Picking me up? Whoever said anything about that?*

"Umm... I could meet you at the airport Mr Ronit. You don't need to go through that trouble," I tried explaining.

"Your office is on my way to the airport and since we are boarding the same flight and we are sort of together, I could do as much?" he said charmingly.

I could almost hear him smile and my inner self beamed for no reason.

"All right then, Mr Ronit. I will see you tomorrow." I smiled.

I postponed the tickets for the rest of them for Monday and informed Ansh about the changes in the plan.

Having finished my packing, I dropped in at my office to see whether things were going fine. I spotted Ansh working on the checklist for my travel.

"Do you think the beach at The Serenity will be available for the venue?" I asked him with a mind full of doubts. My heart prayed for the place to be available. It was like paradise on earth, perfectly suitable for a fantasy wedding.

"Hmm... Just charm your way through with Mr Khaitan, sweetheart! I am sure he will do the job." Ansh was always ready with his encouraging words.

"Yeah!, I guess there is nothing to worry about. I will manage!" I told him as I smiled and got back to my coffee and sandwich.

It was 6:30 p.m. and Mr Ronit would arrive anytime. We had to be at the airport by 7.30. I was checking the time on my watch when I heard a car stop in front of the office.

As I started putting my things together, he entered. Clad in a pair of faded casual denims and a crisp white shirt with sleeves folded up to his arms, he looked as handsome as ever. *Taashi sure was a very lucky girl.*

"Miss Ahaana. Ready to go?" He smiled.

"Yes Mr Ronit." I collected my belongings, gave a quick hug to Ansh and left for the airport.

"I am sorry about the sudden change in plan. Thank you for setting everything up so quickly," he said with a smile as our car zoomed past the others on the road.

"Not a problem. We are often faced with such situations. And since you've agreed to come, I feel it is I who should be thanking you," I said genuinely because had he not come along today, I would really have had a tough time dealing with Mr Khaitan who had a lot of influence, and a little more ego!

Our flight was on time and we reached Goa in less than an hour. Mr Tej from The Serenity received us at the airport.

As we entered the premises, the first thing that came to my mind was that it was huge. I looked at Mr Ronit, who nodded in approval of the place, making me smile and uncross my fingers mentally.

"This place is beautiful, Miss Ahaana! I hope Mr Khaitan can help us settle upon it tomorrow. I can't wait to see the beach. We must get the deal done!" He said looking at me, a boyish grin conquering his handsome face.

"I really hope so too, Mr Ronit!" I exclaimed, echoing his enthusiasm.

Once settled into our rooms, Mr Ronit and I decided to meet for a quick dinner at the dining hall below.

"We seem to be the last ones here, Miss Ahaana, but the place definitely gives a hike to my hunger pangs!" he said as we entered the huge dining hall, which was towards one of the entrances of the resort. It had a split-level setting with a flight of stairs curving towards a platform, which I assumed was made for live performances. Huge windows overlooking the pool added to the aesthetics of the place. The buffet had been already laid and from what the contents looked like, it seemed it was almost wrap up time.

"What would you like to have, Mr Ronit? Some starters first or the main course?"

"First, it is just Ronit. You are planning my wedding and I think we can go on a first-name basis?" he said with a warm smile that touched his eyes, "and I think the main course directly would be a good idea."

"Alright... Ronit," I said with a smile as we set forth for our meal.

As we ate, I told him about Mr Khaitan and his intriguing, yet very pleasant personality.

"So, who all do you have in your family, Ahaana?" Ronit began after we had talked about our schedule for the next day.

"I stay with my parents and my younger brother Krishna; a small family of four," I said fondly.

"That is nice!" he exclaimed and after a small pause, he asked, "How old is Krishna?"

"He is twenty-one, studying engineering. In his final year now!"

"Great! I would like to meet him sometime," Ronit said.

"He might be joining us for the preparations here. He will be having his vacations, and since it is Goa, I don't think he'd be willing to be left behind." I could not help but giggle at the thought of my younger brother helping me rather than attending his parties and other fracas!

Ronit looked at me smiling, as if he could read my thoughts.

"I figure that you share a strong bond with your brother."

I looked up at him and smiled, nodding in agreement.

"A nice and a carefree life, huh?"

"Yeah, you could put it that way! I live life as though it was a dream. You know...?" I raised an eyebrow trying to emphasise on my theory.

"Well... And how do you manage to do that?" He looked at me squarely, a smile touching the corner of his lips.

"It's very simple! Since I lead my life like a dream, happiness always manages to seem like... uh... *dreamlike?* I prefer to ignore the pain and try to feel it did not really get to me, just as in a dream!" The way I said it confused me too, although I hoped Ronit got what it meant.

"That sounds interesting. I like the concept, but I doubt if it would be suitable for people like me."

"Oh, don't bother! Right now you literally have happiness knocking at your door, so live every moment of it, *dream-like!*" I smiled as I said it, though he seemed not to have heard me.

"Ahem..." I cleared my throat, "So tell me about your family. Is it just your parents and you?"

He looked up at me and then simply looked away. I noticed a flicker of emotion in his eyes, but before I could place it, it was gone. Was it sadness or was it something worrying him? I knew I couldn't pry, so I waited for him to go on. He was staring at the bowl of water that held a frail-looking white lily in front of us, his expression unreadable.

"Sometimes I wish Roshan was there!" His words were said so softly that I barely heard him. But I caught the name 'Roshan'.

"Who is Roshan?" I asked, trying to be careful about not delving too much into his personal matters.

"Roshan was my brother. He is no more." The way he said it made something snap inside me. There was pain in his voice and his forehead creased into lines that said that he hid a lot of pain within his heart.

"I.... uh... am so sorry," I whispered, taken aback.

"We lost him when he was just eighteen. He had just got his first bike and was so excited about it that he used to ride it all the time. That night, it was raining. I had returned from London after completing my MBA and had recently joined my father's business. Dad had to stay back for a meeting and since it was raining, I had asked Roshan to come and pick me up. I called him and as I had thought, he was more than willing to help."

I gasped at his revelation while he continued in one breath.

"I'll be there in ten minutes bro! Love you..." were his last words. In the heavy rain, he did not notice a lady crossing the main road. She was in a hurry and had ignored the traffic signal. To save her, he took a deviation, lost control and hit a lorry that came straight at him. The driver of the lorry survived with only a few bruises, but my brother..." Ronit stopped. I noticed his hand tremble. Suddenly, like he had realised my presence, he composed himself.

I saw unshed tears in his eyes and my heart wrenched. I wanted to reach out, to hold his hand and tell him... something, anything that could lessen his pain, even if just a little. But nothing seemed right just then. His loss was done. I could not do anything to help, but maybe just listen. Listening to someone so close being lost in a manner as tragic as this, my heart went out for him. I could not imagine the magnitude of such a loss.

I felt the urge to reach out to this man, who, not more than a few days ago, was a complete stranger. But I simply pushed the thought away, trying my best to give him the space I guess he needed.

"I am so sorry," was all that I could manage to say.

He looked up at me and suddenly said, "So, we shall see each other tomorrow morning at breakfast? The tour of the resort should be fun, Ahaana!" He sounded as though he had said nothing all this while.

"Huh?! Oh yes Ronit! It will be," I said, trying my best to collect myself, shaken with the sudden change in his attitude.

"So, shall we call it a night?"

"Sure, good night Ro... Uh... Mr Ronit," I said as I stood up to leave.

He simply nodded as we got up and walked towards the elevators. I was still too unnerved and his presence inside the elevator was all the more disconcerting. I sighed in relief as the doors gave way to my floor.

As I was about to leave with a formal good night, Ronit said, "Thank you for listening, Ahaana. I am sorry about that," his expression giving away nothing.

Giving him a weak smile, I stepped out. I was about to say something, but was left speechless as the doors of the elevator enveloped him.

The next morning was bright and fresh, although I felt a little tired, considering the hour at which I had slept the previous night. I had been thinking about Ronit and was quite shaken on hearing what his family had gone through. I was to meet him at the dining hall for breakfast and then go on a tour of the wedding venue (which hopefully would be this.)

"Good morning," I heard Ronit's voice from behind as I made my way into the lobby.

I tried not to be nervous since our little 'talk' as I turned to greet him.

Sometimes, when you know that hurt exists at the very core of a person, that in their smile, they are trying to camouflage the scars from within their heart, all you can do is to pretend that what they are trying to hide, is hidden. A smile that hides pain is a defence mechanism of sorts to prevent people from pitying them. But those who are aware of the pain can only help by returning a smile that says all is and will be fine in the future.

I did exactly that as I greeted him with a bright smile.

'Hey! Good morning, Mr Ronit!" I exclaimed cheerfully. I was a bit conscious of my attitude, fearing that I might look too fake. He was wearing beige-coloured shorts and a bright red t-shirt that matched his casual mood, although I kept myself from noticing the taut calf muscles, a clear display of his health routines.

"I hope you slept well last night, Ahaana, and it is *Ronit*," he stressed, smiling broadly and in absolute control of himself. Something about the level of his confidence made me nervous and the fact that he looked drop dead gorgeous did nothing to help. I tried a quick smile as I glanced away consciously.

"I did. Thank you," I hesitated for a split second and then added, "Shall we proceed?"

"Yes! Let us go. I can't wait to see what the beach looks like. I want to picture everything. The stage, the mandap, the guests, *everything*!" he said excitedly.

There was almost a childlike enthusiasm ringing in his voice that made me smile. "Let us grab a quick breakfast and take the tour? Later, by say eleven, Mr Khaitan will be here and we could then discuss the deal with him?"

"Sounds like a plan!" He looked happy as he started walking towards the dining hall. I felt a little edgy just remembering the night before and hoped to God that the place would not remind him of that. I wanted everything to be really special for him. After all, he was the groom and he should definitely be in high spirits – all the time!

In fact, I was hoping for the Guptas to turn up that day, just anyhow, so that Taashi and Ronit could spend some time at the place where they would be getting married. They could create special memories of how they planned their big day here. I was sure Ronit was missing Taashi.

"So, you've always wanted to become an event manager?" Ronit began as we sat down with our plates.

"Yes! I mean, I loved all the glamour and glitter in parties as a child. As I grew up to understand weddings and the emotions surrounding it, I just knew I would be in this business."

"Interesting! And how did you manage to get Ansh into doing that?"

"Umm... It wasn't really a choice that he had!" I giggled. "Basically, we had decided to do something together and since I was so passionate about this, he simply gave in."

"That is a nice partner that you have there!" He smiled.

"Yes!" I said in between mouthfuls. "How do you like the food here?" I enquired.

"It is good! I am sure this seems to be one of the strongest points in choosing this venue."

"Yeah! I am positive that your guests would love the feast here."

He simply nodded his head to that as he took another mouthful.

After breakfast, we headed off to take a look at the beach. It was only 9.30 in the morning and the sun was already scorching. But work had to be done, so we braved the heat and proceeded.

The view, I must say, was breath-taking. The look in my eyes mirrored Ronit's as we stared out at the vast expanse of the ocean before us. The water shone in the broad daylight with the white sand looking soft before our eyes. The waves were small and the sound they made as they splashed softly towards the shore and back, was like a warm melody ringing a lovely musical note. Small star-fishes had washed ashore, making them look like tiny impressions of a star made by a creative child running about. As we neared, they were taken back safely into the waters with the waves again. It was a sight like a dream!

"You must be missing Taashi here," I said as I looked at Ronit relishing the sight before us.

"Oh, yes!" he said softly. "I wonder if she is missing me right now," he added thoughtfully.

"Am sure she must be," I said and smiled.

"So how do you like the venue, Mr Ronit?" I asked as I thought of getting down to business.

"It is just perfect Ahaana. And it is just Ronit please!" He smiled softly, as he looked at me, stressing on the name again.

I caught my breath, as my knees felt almost jelly-like beneath me. *Just his smile can do that to me?* I hesitated once again as I stared at him in awe, at being so aware of himself and so in control of his emotions.

"All that is left is to have the deal finalised and the rest is for you to decide. The planning of the grace and grandeur with which Taashi and I will be united forever is now under your control."

My heart danced at the thought that he depended on me. His playful words drew a nervous laugh out of me. But again, the confidence that he showed right now made me want to get started with the wedding preparations right away!

"So, is this a love marriage or an arranged marriage, Ronit? I hope you don't mind me asking that though." I shifted uncomfortably at the thought that I might be prying, but that uncertainty was gone when he smiled and answered, "It is a very thoughtfully arranged marriage Ahaana!" I don't know if I was right or wrong, but I thought I caught a hint of mockery in his tone. Eyeing him curiously, I waited for him to elaborate.

"Well, I was not willing to get married as yet, but Mom insists that I must, considering that I am already twenty-eight. My parents met the Guptas at a wedding of a common friend where they got a chance to see Taashi. They decided that we were a perfect match and arranged my meeting with her. I guess I liked her too and now we are getting married." He put his hands up in the air in the most theatrical way and said, "It has been just three weeks since we met and in four months we shall be life partners!" he exclaimed, smiling down at me.

"Wow!" I said aloud before I could stop myself. "That is an exciting story. If only finding soul-mates was this easy for the rest of us." I rolled my eyes, trying to match his ardour.

He laughed at that and said, "Why? I think you and Ansh make a really good pair."

"What?" I was more than soberly loud. "Oh, no! Ansh and I are not a couple. We are just *really* good friends."

"Oh, I am so sorry. I thought the two of you were together."

"That is alright! He is my best buddy and we have been that way ever since I have known him. We just haven't seen each other in any manner different than that and I guess we like it that way," I said as a matter of fact.

"Hmm," he said eyeing me curiously.

I felt uncomfortable under his gaze, but tried my best to maintain a straight face.

"Ronit, I think we must get back inside now. I need to get some papers arranged before we meet Mr Khaitan. You could explore the place if you like."

"I think I will go back in as well Ahaana. I have a few calls to make and maybe check on Taashi to see what she's up to." He winked.

"Okay. I will see you at the lobby in an hour then?"

He nodded as he led the way back into the hotel. While he made his way towards the elevator, I walked over to the reception to grab a catalogue of The Serenity with its maps and details. This would give me a clear idea about how to utilise the venue to its best. I also had to check upon Mr Pinto, the manager, to see if he would be joining us for the meeting with Mr Khaitan.

It was 11.30 as I reached the lobby, the papers in my hand. I looked around for Ronit and found him at a distance, talking to a young man. I checked my watch and waited patiently for Mr Khaitan to arrive.

Ronit came up as I was taking a final look at the papers. We both hoped and were almost sure that the deal would be finalised.

After about ten minutes, we were joined by Mr Khaitan and after a brief exchange of greetings, we settled down to work.

Mr Khaitan was a known figure in the area and he drew much attention. An amicable personality, he was kind-hearted and always ready to help.

Mr Pinto, the manager also joined us.

"Welcome to The Serenity, sir. It is a pleasure to have you here," said Mr Pinto as he shook hands with Mr Khaitan.

"Thank you, Mr Pinto," Mr Khaitan said smiling.

"Ahaana, so it is yet another grandeur you are planning!" Mr Khaitan started the conversation in a pretty light manner.

"Yes sir." I smiled as I exchanged looks with Ronit. "This is Mr Ronit Malthotra, a very humble and respectable businessman Mr Deepak Malthotra's son, and a very modest person himself."

"It is nice to meet you, Mr Ronit." Mr Khaitan bent forward and shook hands with Ronit.

"A pleasure to meet you too, Mr Khaitan," Ronit returned with a smile.

I could not help but notice the power exuding Ronit's personality and how he was comfortable in his own skin. Somehow, his control and charisma ignited a forcible strength, making me believe that I could make this wedding one of a kind. Straightening up, I got down to the mission of securing The Serenity into our bag.

It is often believed that something desired from the deepest core of the heart actually materializes at some point of time. I am one such believer. And the belief grew stronger after Mr Khaitan helped us get the dates booked at The Serenity.

Delighted at the thought of having the venue finalized, we both beamed at each other as Mr Khaitan left. We were happy at the success of the deal. Ronit rang to inform his fiancé and his parents while I informed Ansh.

"Guess what?" I said as I tried hard to hide the excitement.

"You did it!"

"We did it!" We exclaimed in unison.

"Yes, we did it Ansh!" I couldn't hide my joy. It meant a lot to do a high scale wedding at The Serenity and it was going to add one more feather to our cap - one more success story!

"I knew you would, Ahaana! This is great." He sounded so excited that I could almost imagine him jump at the other end.

"Thank youuuu!" I sang, giggling.

"We shall meet tomorrow at the resort. How is Mr Ronit treating you? I hope you are enjoying your time there. He seemed like a nice chap to me."

"Aah yes! He is nice and friendly, and no, I am not getting bored. I think I will start planning while I wait here for you guys to arrive. By what time will you be here? Have you confirmed the timings with Taashi and both their fathers?"

"Yes, I've confirmed with Mr Deepak Malhotra. But I am unable to get through to Taashi or her father. I have the tickets ready. I have just been trying to reach them. Hey, why don't you ask Mr Ronit to call them and inform me?"

"All right, I will do that."

After I hung up, I looked around to see if Ronit was there or if he was still on his call. Insead, I found him sitting across from where I was, staring blankly at his cell phone. Not happy… not too worried either… just blank. I went up to him.

"Have you spoken to Miss Taashi and her parents?"

"I spoke to my dad!" he said absently.

"And Miss Taashi?"

"I don't know. She is not taking my call. She must be occupied with something," he said. Disconcertment was pretty evident in that tone.

She must be busy? Really?

"Why don't you try calling Mr Gupta? I had a word with Ansh just now. He wanted to inform them about tomorrow's schedule, but he hasn't been able to get through. Maybe you could let us know?"

"All right, I will inform him." Saying this, he dialled Mr Gupta's number.

His brows had freckled in a very weird manner and he was making a childlike swell on his cheeks while he impatiently waited for Mr Gupta to answer the call.

He caught me off guard and I looked away immediately, hiding the sheepish grin that spread wide across my face.

"What is so funny?" He gaped at me awkwardly. "My fiancé and her father are not taking my calls. Don't you think *you* should be equally anxious? And you are finding this funny?" As he said this, his brows almost danced on his forehead.

I burst out laughing.

"I know I should be worried, both for my business and my clients. But your expressions could not be ignored." And I convulsed into fits of laughter as I figured that the dancing of his eyebrows was happening quite involuntarily.

My laughter seemed to ease his tension as he broke into a grin, making me laugh hysterically. We didn't realise that we were attracting attention until someone commented – "Honeymoon times are the best." The statement caught us both off guard, making me nervously straighten myself while Ronit ended up coughing.

"Let me try her number again," Ronit said as he began dialing Tashi's number.

At the same instant, my phone rang, making me jump, distracting me from the thoughts going on in my wrecked head! Ansh's name blinked on the screen of my cell phone.

"Hey Ansh!" I said absently.

"Hey Ahaana. I just happened to speak to Mr Gupta. He said that it would take them a while to get back to Bangalore. Miss Taashi has some urgent work. I don't think it will be fruitful to go all the way to Goa with only Mr Deepak Malhotra. What do you say?"

"Huh?! Are you serious? This is so immature of Taashi! If Ronit can take time off, why can't she, that too for her own wedding?" I said bitterly.

"What is wrong with you, Ahaana? I think someone is getting personal here!"

And before he got any weird hints, I immediately composed myself, silently cursing myself for giving away my recent wayward thoughts.

"Uh... I am sorry! I will inform Mr Ronit about the change of plans. I think in that case we will get back by Sunday morning."

"Yes, that would be better."

"Okay, I shall call you once I reach Bangalore." And with that, we hung up.

I walked towards Ronit who was looking more puzzled than ever. Remembering our previous laughter riot, I smiled.

"Hey, they won't be coming!" we said together.

"Yes, I see you are already informed. Did Ansh call you?" Ronit asked.

"He did. There is a delay in their plans and they won't be getting time until next week, right?"

"Yeah!"

I sensed uncertainty in his tone and I guess my expressions conveyed the same to him. But Ronit preferred to keep his worry to himself and I decided not to indulge into it any further.

It was already half past two and we both simultaneously remembered that we had not had lunch yet. Ronit was still a little distant and thus I thought better than to pry in his personal matters. We decided to order some Chinese and stopped at The Shoots for lunch.

"I am sorry, Ahaana. Now you guys will have to plan again for the next weekend," Ronit apologised.

"That is all right Ronit. These little things keep happening. What matters most is that we got a perfect location." I beamed and tried sounding enthusiastic, but the truth was that we would have to redo a lot of things because of changes in the plan.

For a while after that, there was no exchange of words between us. He seemed pre-occupied and not willing to interfere. I shifted my thoughts in making mental notes of various decors that may look good in these aesthetics. The wedding after all was all that I was supposed to think about, right?!

"I was wondering if we could fly back tonight," Ronit asked suddenly.

"Huh!? Uh… sure! I will check post lunch if there are any seats available for the evening flight."

"That would be great," he said. His voice revealed neither enthusiasm nor worry. I could sense something amiss, but I didn't want to be intrusive. Once done with the lunch, Ronit decided to head back to his room and do some follow up while I went ahead to put us on the next flight.

I managed to fetch us two seats on the evening flight. We still had quite a few hours in hand and I went on to explore the resort. Walking outdoors was not an option, as I didn't want to get myself tanned under the scorching sun.

There was a lounge at the far end inside the resort and I decided to go there. As I walked inside, I couldn't help but admire its aqua decor with long glass windows overlooking the beach. Tinted blue tiles synchronized with white ones to form a pathway with a stream of water running down right at the centre of the room. The path was covered with toughened glass for people to walk over.

With a mojito in one hand, I took one of the seats and breathed in the freshness, as a waft of salty air filled the area. I took a sip and relaxed against the backrest. Closing my eyes, I savoured its taste and enjoyed the coolness running down my throat. It was a good thing that the venue was finalized. Now the only thing left was to wait for Taashi and her parents to give their opinion. But I was sure that they too would love the place.

While I was busy thinking, I did not notice Ronit walking into the lounge.

Ronit

"I wonder what is going on?" Ronit grumbled to himself as he entered the lounge. It had been almost an hour since his last call to Taashi and her behaviour had been inexplicably absurd. It was her wish to plan the wedding in Goa and now she wasn't here. Moreover, she did not care to mention the reason why. She was not with her dad, that he knew. They had flown in from Bombay the day before and were planning to fly here by next day morning. But now, only her dad was in Bangalore and Taashi, she simply said she wouldn't be able to make it. He didn't understand what bothered her and the only way that he could get his answers was when he would meet her. He was not used to getting dismissed this way and that surely bothered him. It was not ego; it was more about what was going on in her mind.

Frustrated, he walked over to the bar counter and ordered a drink. Absently, he checked his watch. It was only half past three and there were still about five hours until he could speak to Taashi.

As he waited for his order to arrive, he noticed that the lounge could actually be a nice place for a pre-wedding party. But again, he mocked at himself as he remembered Taashi's abrupt refusal to come. Trying to ignore his thoughts, he allowed himself to get distracted by the interesting juggle of bottles by the bartender before him. As he looked up at the mirror behind the bartender, he spotted Ahaana sitting by herself at a distance, pre-occupied.

For a moment, things changed within his head. He felt there was a certain charm that she possessed which was something he had not experienced before. The unmatched sincerity she had for her work was extraordinary. One day was all that he had spent with her and it had been so easy to be himself around her.

He sighed as his thoughts returned to Taashi. He simply could not understand what was going on in her mind. He did want to respect her feelings, but he could do so only if he knew what they were. Agreed, it had been only a short while since they had met, and he also knew it would take time for them to really understand each other, but he was at least trying.

He spent a little while there quietly, lost in his own complications. He looked towards Ahaana once again and felt guilty for his rude behaviour at lunch. He contemplated going to her, but then kept to his place preferring not to disturb her. A smile found its way on his face as he guessed she must have already started planning the wedding.

At around five, he decided to get back to his room and prepare to leave for the airport.

As he stood up to leave, he glanced over towards Ahaana and still found her engrossed in the book she held. Thinking better, he walked towards her.

"Hey," he said softly so that he did not surprise her.

"Oh, hi! I did not see you coming."

"I have been around for a while. Saw you, but did not want to bother you," he said, smiling softly.

"Oh! I am sorry. I was just making notes about the preparations."

"That is alright Ahaana. I was just heading back to my room. We will be leaving in about half an hour?"

"Yes, yes! That will be fine. It is an hour's drive from here to the airport."

"Okay! I will see you at the lobby in a while."

"Sure," she said as she stood up to leave.

"Hey Ahaana!" He called before he could stop himself.

"Yes, Mr Ronit?"

He noticed the formal tone of her voice.

"Well, I just wanted to say I am sorry about these unnecesary complications and also for being unattentive. There were so many things going on in my head."

"You don't have to give an explanation. I understand," she said smiling sweetly.

"Thank you," he said as a smile found its way to the corners of his mouth. The warmth of her smile did wonders for his mood.

As Ronit and Ahaana boarded their flight, tiredness washed over them. While all Ahaana needed was the cosy comfort of her bed and a good night's sleep, Ronit felt just the opposite. He was wide awake and gearing up to meet Taashi with a mission to figure out what was going on. She had not returned any of his calls and he had stopped trying. He had decided to go to her place and sort matters out.

When they landed at Bangalore, it was already ten at night. He insisted upon dropping Ahaana to her place.

"Thank you, Ronit."

"It was my pleasure, Ahaana."

"Please do inform me about your plans for the next visit to the venue with Miss Taashi and both your families. We need all your opinions and suggestions before we begin our work."

"I understand Ahaana. I am sorry about the delay. I will definitely revert to you at the earliest."

"Thank you and good night," she said as she turned to leave.

"Good night, Ahaana," he replied as he sat behind the wheels and without wasting a minute, drove towards Taashi's residence.

It had been almost five minutes since he had been standing at Taashi's door. He had tried calling the landline, but it had gone unanswered. Although it was eleven, it was not normal for the Gupta family to retire to bed at this hour. They usually stayed up late.

I'd better call Mr Gupta, he thought as he dialled.

"Hello!" said a loud voice at the other end. Ronit held the phone away for a second as the piercing noise made him recoil.

"Mr Gupta, Ronit here," he said loudly so that he could be audible. "I am at your place right now and want to meet Taashi, but no one is answering the door. Would she be in there?"

"Oh Ronit, hi!" There was a pause as the noise faded at the other end. "Sorry, I was not able to hear you properly," said a more audible Mr Gupta. "Taashi was at home when we left. She must be there," he said confidently.

"I have been standing at your door since the last ten minutes. No one seems to be in," he argued and got a little worried about the prospects. Was she hurt? Should he break in? Or, maybe she is elsewhere and her parents didn't know?

"Hang on, let me call her."

"I have been trying her number from Goa since afternoon and have not been able to get through even once. Is there a problem, Mr Gupta? Should I break in?" he asked, a little more worried now.

"Oh no, I am sure you wouldn't have to do that. She was very much there at home when we left and she didn't mention anything about going anywhere. Just wait, I will be there in ten minutes." His worry reflected in her father's voice as well. Since Mr Gupta was a man of strict principles and limited display of feelings, witnessing the concern in his voice was something new.

Mr Gupta arrived in less than ten minutes. They acknowledged each other's presence with a mere nod while the worried father got busy unlocking the front door of the house. As they entered, the house looked completely deserted. The lights were out and as Ronit stepped in, he suddenly stumbled upon something with a loud thud. Mr Gupta was quick to switch on the lights. Ronit had bumped into a ceramic pillar. They headed to where Taashi's room was.

"Taashi?" Mr Gupta called out.

"Taashi!" he called again, louder this time, but there was no response.

This did not make them feel comfortable and they both rushed towards Taashi's bedroom. As they threw open the door, they found the room engulfed in darkness. Mr Gupta turned the lights on and as it flooded the room, they were struck with its emptiness. For a second Mr Gupta seemed relieved of his worst fears.

As they turned to leave, Ronit noticed a small piece of paper with a glass working as a paper-weight, at what he thought was her study.

While he approached it, Mr Gupta turned around and noticed the same. As he unfolded the paper, a strange feeling crept into his mind. He knew something was definitely *not* right. With knitted brows, he began reading aloud what he presumed to be Taashi's handwriting.

Dear Dad,

I am sorry for leaving abruptly in the midst of all the excitement. But I had no other way to get away from what you had decided for me. I do not wish to marry Ronit!

Ronit paused as he looked up at her father who was staring at him like he already knew what was written in that piece of paper. Ronit looked down at the letter again, while Taashi's father mustered a clueless expression, worry surfacing on his wrinkled features all over again. He stepped forward in an attempt to take the letter from Ronit, but instead Ronit continued,

I am not saying that Ronit is not nice, Dad. I am just not ready for marriage yet. I have my dreams, which I want to work for. And I want to marry only after I get the right person for me.

I know you do not approve of my decision and would force me to do otherwise. Therefore, I thought it's better to go to my friend's place in Mumbai.

I am sorry to have upset you, but this is about my life, Daddy. I have been trying to tell you, but you would not listen. So it had to be this way. I know I can't undo the harm I have done, but I know you will forgive me.

I will ask for Ronit's forgiveness myself. I know I have no right to hurt him and I'm sorry for being the reason of his pain. I do regret this.
Please forgive me Dad.

Yours,

Taashi

For a while Ronit did not know how to react. Yes, she can live her life the way she wants to, but she could have conveyed that to him earlier, right? He felt cheated and could not bear standing there for another minute. Anger threatened to creep in as he looked at Taashi's father. He searched his eyes for any answers, but found them avoiding his questioning glance.

Ronit took a step back and began leaving with a straight look that exuded nothing but repentance. As he neared the door, he heard Mr Gupta say, "Ronit, I am sorry!" There was sympathy in his voice.

Instead of looking back, Ronit walked back to his car and drove away.

All her words and actions came flooding through the gates of his memories of the past month. Why hadn't he read her expressions earlier and why couldn't she just tell him frankly, he hissed through gritted teeth. A rush of questions conquered his mind, but all without any answers. He then decided that he did not want to think about it now. Nothing mattered. Dejection was all he felt.

Exhausted, Ronit turned off the lights of his room and sat in the dark, trying to fight back the betrayal. But he knew how to get a grip on himself. He still had to give the news to his parents who would perhaps be more upset than he was. He had to take charge of the situation now and not let anything get out of hand. Taashi did not want to marry him and that was all right. It was her life and she had decided. But his life also had him as the decision maker. And today, he decided to let go. He would steer his life whichever way he wanted…

Some Mondays ideally seem to explain why the saying 'Monday blues' was coined, today specifically being one of those. Work was just not happening. I'd already had three cups of coffee and yet my mind was completely inactive.

I was at my desk, working on the themes for Ronit Malhotra's wedding, a list of pointers before me. I had not got a call from him yet about our next visit to the venue and it had already been two days since our return. I chewed the metal casing of the tiny eraser on my pencil as I fidgeted with my phone, contemplating whether to call him myself or not. I exhaled, sighing.

Ansh was awaiting Ronit's affirmation for the flight bookings. Unable to delay the matter any further, I picked up the phone and dialled Ronit's number.

As the phone rang, I restlessly tapped the pencil on my desk. It went on a no reply and just as I was about to try one more time, Ansh approached my desk.

"Any word from Mr Ronit?" he asked.

"Not yet. I did try, but he didn't answer." Just then, my phone rang. It was him!

"Mr Ronit," I said in a matter of fact voice as Ansh walked away.

"Hi Ahaana," he said in a voice that was different than how I remembered him talking.

I cleared my throat, but before I could say anything, he startled me by saying, "Before you begin Ahaana, I wanted to inform you that the wedding has been called off."

My jaw dropped as I took a minute for the information to sink in. I tried to find something to say, but was rendered speechless. "Oh, I am so sorry," was all that I managed.

"It is all right. I guess it just wasn't meant to be." And he stopped at that.

I fumbled with words as his silence made me uncomfortable. It was difficult to figure out what to say, because it seemed like he had already accepted the fact.

"I don't know what to say Ronit. I am really sorry."

There was a long pause at the other end making me shift uncomfortably. I heard him exhale.

"Uh… No worries Ahaana. I am sorry." There was a sudden shift in his voice, taking complete control. *How did he do that?*

"I am extremely sorry, for you guys must have started all the planning. You took time out for the venue visit. All your efforts, wasted. I sincerely apologize for that."

"No Ronit. It is not as big a deal as it must be for you. Please don't even bother about us in that regard. I hope you have taken it well. I cannot say much except that sometimes funny things happen to even the best of people." I tried my best.

"Thank you for taking away the burden of guilt that kept me from calling you. I am sorry again," he said formally, but politely.

"Not to mention Ronit. What are friends for!"

"Thank you once again Ahaana."

And with another nod, I hung up, not knowing whether we would ever be in touch again.

I stared at my desk, lost in my thoughts. Everything had seemed so perfect between them. But then I realised that I did find her behaviour awkward for a person who was going to be married soon, but it was not like I could imagine that the wedding could be called off, especially when everything was planned and decided. I cringed at the thought of what Ronit must be going through.

While still lost in my thoughts, I was suddenly startled with a tap on my shoulders. I looked up to see Mishka and Ansh, both standing over my desk, worry visibly spread across their faces.

"What is wrong with you? We have been calling out your name for so long," Ansh asked with concern in his voice.

"Is something wrong dear? Who was it on the phone?" Mishka's troubled voice added.

"Hey guys, I am sorry. It's nothing. I was just pre-occupied."

"What happened, Ahaana? I think I left you speaking to Mr Ronit a while ago. Is something wrong? Does he want a change of venue or something?" Ansh's tone got hyper.

"On the contrary, he has called off his wedding," I murmured in a sad voice.

"What!? Why? What happened?" they both exclaimed simultaneously.

"I don't know. He just called to say that the wedding is off."

"Oh, that is terrible," Mishka said in a sad voice.

"That is really sad. I wonder what could have happened!" Ansh said genuinely.

"Yeah!" I just muttered and excused myself.

I needed some fresh air for my crazily cluttered head to clear. A while ago there was so much to plan and execute, and now suddenly, nothing. It was not just about the business, there were also emotions involved. Weird emotions that made me want to call Ronit, to know what went wrong. But then, I held myself back.

With a cool breeze and a possibility of rain, the weather was nice and cool outside. But the emotions within me made everything seem dull.

Inside, Ansh and Mishka were busy cancelling all the arrangements and appointments. That reminded me to call Mr Pinto, the manager at The Serenity and cancel the booking we had made. I had to inform Mr Khaitan as well.

I picked up the phone and set about the tasks rather forlornly.

It was my day off. I was relaxing at home when the phone rang. It was a number I didn't recognise.

"Hey Ahaana!" a rather familiar voice said.

"Hello... yes?"

"It's Rahul!"

"Oh, what a surprise!" I grinned. Rahul was a good friend from college. He had called after almost three years. Ansh kept me updated about him though. We three had been buddies in college.

"I am in town. Reached yesterday and had been meaning to call you."

"That's great!"

"How are you? It's been ages since I met you. Tell me, how's work and how's life?" he started in his usual, familiar carefree manner.

"I am doing great. Busy with work and life, just like everyone else."

"Ansh keeps telling me about the fun you guys have at work!"

"Yes, we do. How are things at your end?" Rahul had joined his dad's family business of textiles.

"It is hectic, very hectic actually. We have this client that requires me to travel to UK almost once every month and I am getting tired of it. I am in town actually, but only for two days. Leaving tomorrow."

"You're here? Oh, I wish we could meet up."

"I know. I just came down for a friend's wedding. In fact, I was hoping to meet you guys there, because I thought you would be the event managers for it."

"Thank you for that, but not every event in the city is planned by us," I giggled to which he just laughed.

"So, anyone special you want to update me about?" I asked.

"Hmm! Is it the friend or the event manager asking?" I could hear the smirk in his voice.

"The *friend*," I said, stressing on the word.

Rahul giggled. "Not yet sweetheart! That would have to wait! What about you?"

"Well, nothing's happening as yet!"

"And is Ansh in the league as well?"

"Yes, pretty much!"

"I really wanted to meet you guys, but it seems all my time will be taken up with this wedding. And I need to rush back early tomorrow," he said.

"It would have been so nice to see you. But no problem, I am sure we will get an opportunity soon," I said.

There was a pause at the other end and I guessed something was fishy. So I poked him again, "Why do I have a feeling that you want to tell me something? Come on! Out with it, Rahul!"

"Huh?" he sounded taken aback, which confirmed my hunch. "I'm waiting," I said in a singsong voice.

"Like hell! It's been ages and you still haven't let go of your dominance."

"Oh my god! So there is someone. Tell me now!" I said all excited.

I heard him laugh as he gave in saying, "All right lady, I will tell you. Her name is Meera and I met her at a get-together at one of my official meets." And he stopped at that.

"Rahul, I don't need a synopsis. Tell me more. How did it start, everything..."

"Okay, okay!" he said and continued, "I met Meera at an official get-together. However Ahaana, it was a very different start."

He paused and I waited for him to go on.

"I saw her first and there was something magical about her that literally drew me her way. I simply couldn't take my eyes off her and there was just one thought screaming in my head – to go and meet her, to hear her voice!

"I thought of introducing myself to her right then and as I went ahead to do so, I saw her approaching a man. He was tall and handsome, wearing dark shades, dressed formally. Taking his arm, she moved ahead. I held back, realising she was not alone, and quite possibly was married."

I smiled and waited for him to go on, not affected by the small dramatic stir he caused, knowing that their love story had a happy ending.

"The same night as I was leaving, I saw her again. This time she was alone and I wondered where her husband was. I was standing outside the auditorium premises and she was waiting at the main entrance. I looked around, trying to see if I could spot him, when I suddenly saw him arm in arm with another girl.

"It was pitch dark outside and he was wearing the shades again, which was ridiculous. Finding it absurd, I went to the security guard, hoping to know who they were."

"He informed me that they were from an orphanage and had been invited by one of my bosses to meet someone. Apparently, the man in shades was blind and the girl who held him was the manager of the orphanage. The beautiful stranger was also one of the residents at the orphanage. I felt a slight prick in my heart for the girl. There was something about her that made me want to know her better.

"So the next day, I went to the orphanage and stood right across the building, trying to see if I could see her from there.

Coincidentally, she appeared at the entrance. Gathering all my courage, I decided to approach her.

"As I began crossing the road towards the gate, the awkwardness of just walking over to a girl made me stop. But I didn't realize that I had stopped right in the middle of the road until a car hit me. I was thrown to the ground with the impact."

"What? Why didn't you mention this? Was it very bad? Oh god Rahul, I am so sorry!" I said, shocked and worried.

"Hey relax Ahaana. That was months back. And I am perfectly fine now," he said smiling. "The next thing I knew when I opened my eyes was that I was at a hospital with a fractured leg and arm. I thanked god that I was at least alive.

"I got to know that a girl called Meera had brought me there. I waited impatiently, hoping that she would visit me.

"And she did come, Ahaana. She was so beautiful. It was at that moment that I felt my heart flutter and all the pain vanished. It was love at first sight." He left a breath, sighing with a smile.

It was such a beautiful feeling. I felt so happy for him. "But how did she end up falling in love with you?" I asked him.

"Well, when she had come to see me, she held a bunch of flowers, and said she was sorry. When I asked her why, she smiled and said, that had she not been standing on the opposite side of the road, the mishap wouldn't have happened at all. That's when I just knew her heart. Since then, we spoke every day, met more and more, and treaded upon the road of love."

It was rare to hear such words from a guy, but Rahul was like that, the guy who knew and valued emotions. I was so happy for him.

Rahul told me that they were planning to get married this year. I was almost teary-eyed as I fell in love with their love story.

As I hung up, I was overwhelmed with the beauty of love and the intensity it brought within our hearts.

I had gone out for a walk in the evening, after a lazy day at home. But when I came back, I noticed a sudden chaos at home. Mom was talking cheerfully over the phone at the peak of her voice while Dad was talking loudly on another call. I saw Krishna gaping at them. He had a broad grin pasted on his face. *What's going on in here,* I wondered as I walked over to Krish with questioning eyes.

"Jia is getting married!" he exclaimed.

Whoa! "What?" I shrieked happily.

Jia was our maasi's daughter. Mom has only one sister, Raadha Maasi and we are very close to her family. Radha Maasi has two kids, Jia and Saurabh and they are all settled in Mumbai. Jia is about the same age as me while Saurabh is a year younger than Krish. The four of us got along really well and now, listening to this news had filled my household with a fervour of festivity.

Gosh! Love really is *in the air.* I giggled at my own thoughts as I immediately took out my phone and dialled Jia's number, anxious to get all the information myself.

I waited impatiently for her to answer the call but it kept ringing and went on a no-reply. I tried again, but in vain. Guessing that she must be busy, I walked towards Mom, who by that time, had just ended her call. She looked at me, beaming with excitement.

"Jia is getting married!!" I cheerfully hugged her. This was such a wonderful piece of news. It would be the first wedding of our generation.

"Tell me all about it. How did everything happen? Did Jia know the guy? What is his name? Where is he from?" I threw a volley of questions at my mother, who burst into laughter, gauging my anxiety.

"You kids!" She giggled. "It is an arranged marriage, Ahaana. And the boy's name is Rishabh. Why don't you ask Jia? She must be waiting for your call," Mom said lovingly.

"Of course! I did try, but she didn't answer the call. Okay wait, I shall try again." I dialled Jia's number and this time my call was on waiting. *Well! Well!* I thought and dialled again, grinning at Mom.

"Ahaana!" An ecstatic Jia answered the call.

"So you are already on long calls with your to-be-hubby, huh?" I said teasingly.

"Ahaanaaa…" she said in a sing-song voice, clearly blushing.

"You are getting married sweetheart!" and for a second I was unable to control my emotions. My voice cracked and I inhaled as Jia said softly, "I am getting married Ahaana and I am in love. I am so happy. My god, there is so much that I want to tell you." I could sense Jia's happiness and excitement as I fought back my own tears of happiness and giggled, wishing I could give her a big hug.

"Come on, tell me everything!" I said excitedly.

"Well, I met him for the first time two months ago…"

"What? Two months and I get to know now?" I complained, cutting her short, pouting like she could see.

"It just got official now, Ahaana. I am so sorry I couldn't inform you immediately."

"Okay whatever. Now tell me about Rishabh. Where is he from? What does he do? I don't know anything." I frowned.

"Okay, then at least let me speak." We giggled and she went on. "He is also from Mumbai and is the only son of his parents. He did his MBA from the USA and is planning to get settled in New York post marriage. It is completely an arranged marriage sweetie and now," she paused for a second, "I think, I just might have fallen in love," she said dreamily.

"Awww.... Jia! I am so happy for you." First it was Rahul and now, my sister.

"Ahaana, next weekend is my engagement and I want you here!"

"That goes without saying, sweetheart. I will be there ahead of time."

We landed at the Chhatrapati Shivaji International Airport at around noon on Wednesday. The weather was bright and sunny while the air was a tad humid. I craned my neck up, screening the crowd in the arrivals section, trying to spot Radha Maasi or Saurabh. Suddenly, I heard a shrill voice screaming out my name and at once knew it was Jia's.

Lean and tall, she outshined in the small crowd gathered at the arrivals area. She had a wide grin spread across her face as she waved at us with both her hands swaying wildly above her head. I waved back grinning broadly.

"Mom, you go meet them. I will take care of the luggage," I said.

"Alright. Let Krish help you. I'll go meet Radha. But where is he?" We both looked for Krish and realised that he was already talking to Saurabh. Giggling at his impatience, I beckoned Mom to go as well and walked towards the conveyor belt. Waiting impatiently for my luggage, I looked towards Jia again. I spotted Radha Maasi behind her and waved at her. It was really sweet of them to have come over to receive us.

I finally spotted our red suitcases and got prepared to lift them up, fretting the weight that they carried. I managed to pick them up somehow. As I put it onto the trolley, Krish rushed in offering a helping hand. *Brothers!*

"Hey, sorry sis," he said, embarrassed.

"It's ok. I didn't expect them to come so soon either," I said, smiling at him.

"Let's go! They are waiting," Krish said, already taking the trolley from me and walking towards them.

I ran towards Jia, embracing her in a bear hug!

"Congratulations!" I sang aloud, not even attempting to hide my joy.

"Thank you so much!" she squealed as she hugged me back. Radha Maasi smiled from behind us as I enveloped her in a tight hug as well.

"You have grown taller Ahaana and so beautiful," she said fondly.

"Thank you, Maasi. You have lost so much weight!" I exclaimed cheerfully as I quickly examined her from top to bottom and saw her cheeks go red. This was what she was famous for – her blushing – and seeing that, all of us giggled.

She shied away and smiled. Catching up like old times, we were soon on our way towards Radha Maasi's house.

After settling down, Jia took me to her room for a private chat. There was so much to know. Her room was the same as I remembered the last time I was here, a glimpse of a fairy-tale. The walls were a light shade of pink with one corner dedicated towards her passion for photograhy, flaunting pictures of her, with her friends, with Saurabh, her parents and also a picture with me. She still had tiny Disney stickers from our childhood days, stuck on her laminated wardrobe. I smiled at the flash of memories as I realised that now the time had come... she was really getting married.

"So, how is it going?" I asked her brightly.

"It is a whole new world Ahaana. Rishabh is soooooo cute."

I smiled at the way she said it. It was so nice to see her glowing with happiness.

"Wait, I will show you something," she said as she almost jumped up and went to her desk. She removed a box, the size of an encyclopaedia. The top of it was painted with a beautiful rose and over it was written, '*For the one who has made my life a love story*'.

"Wow! Is that done by him?" I asked, my eyes shining bright.

"Open it!" Jia was making it sound so full of suspense.

As I opened the box, I took in a sharp breath as I saw a beautiful sketch of Jia. It was almost life-like and below it was signed 'Rishabh's Jia'.

"Oh my god, Jia!" I gasped in wonder. "This is spectacular. He sketched this for you? It is so beautiful." I ran short of words. This guy seemed just the right person for her. An amazingly emotional person that she was, gestures like this was what she had always wanted from her partner.

"Isn't it awesome?" she cooed. "Rishabh gave it to me last weekend, when he actually proposed to me formally on his knees!" she squealed in delight as I giggled, unbelievingly.

"So cute," I said looking fondly at her.

"I know! I am so happy that I have found the guy I had been looking for. He is totally amazing and loves me very much."

"I am very happy for you Jia. I really wanted you to get the perfect guy and he seems so right for you. And seeing this," I said pointing at the sketch, "... he is almost godsent!"

"Oh, he is," she replied, dreamily, making me grin as both of us giggled like little girls.

"But you know what Ahaana," she paused, "I am a little nervous. Leaving Mom and Dad, the entire aspect of changing everything I've ever had."

"I can understand sweetie. But don't worry. Everything will fall in place with time. Plus, look at the brighter side of it. You are still going to be in Mumbai."

"Yeah, but that is only for a while. Then we will be moving to the US," she said nervously.

"By the time you will be moving, you would have already got to know Rishabh and his family. Trust me, you will be just fine!"

"Oh Ahaana, thank god you are here."

With that, she suddenly began to cry. I immediately went and took her into my arms. I knew she was nervous. The strange feelings of happiness of finding the love of your life, mixed with the fear of leaving everything that you had ever known and cared for behind – it was all a part of this.

"Shhh!" I soothed her. "We are all there for you dear. And you have found a great guy who loves you a lot."

She looked at me and smiled, composing herself. Her anxiety was evident. I consoled her and it was a while before we got back to our usual flip repartee. She showed me her engagement outfit. It was stunningly designed. It was different shades of pink with an elegant velvet lehenga in purple, teamed up with detailed embroidery in copper along its borders.

"Wow! You are going to look breathtakingly beautiful in it, my girl!" I beamed at her.

"Thank you Ahaana!" She smiled sheepishly as she hugged her ensemble.

The next two days were completely exhaustive and yet full of fun. We all participated in the preparations for the engagement and welcomed the guests.

It was Saturday and the engagement ceremony was the same evening. I had got myself a lehenga for the occasion. It had royal blue and copper colours in perfect combination with a dash of mirror work, making it just right. I could not wait to wear it since it had been a while since I had got a chance to don Indian ethnic wear.

I wanted to be with Jia while her make-up artist was to prepare her for the event. Thus I decided to get ready early while Jia was still away at the salon for some last minute pre-make-up services. It took me about half an hour to get myself clad in my lehenga and put on some light make-up. As I tried to pleat my dupatta, I heard some chaos outside my room and guessed that Jia must have returned from the parlour. I rushed out towards the door.

"Jia, get dressed quick beta. We hardly have time," I heard Radha Maasi as I opened the door of my room and stepped out. I was a little taken aback and embarrassed when heads gradually turned to see me.

"Wow Ahaana! You look amazing," Jia said smiling at me lovingly.

"Thank you, sweetheart! But I can't wait to see *you* all set."

"Arre Ahaana, you are looking very pretty beta," Maasi said brimming with motherly love.

"Thank you Maasi," I said as I approached my mother and Krish.

"Wow Ahaana, you look gorgeous," he said smiling generously.

"Thanks Krish."

"Now let me look at you, young lady!" said Dad, rising and holding me by my shoulders. "The most beautiful girl, second to your mother of course." He grinned as he enveloped me in his strong arms.

"I am sure to get many proposals for you today Ahaana!" cooed Mom.

"Don't even get there, Mom!"

"Don't you think so Radha?" my mother continued, promptly ignoring my plea.

"Absolutely! I think the next big bash is coming soon," Radha Maasi teased.

I sighed at the non-stop playful teasing and looked towards Jia for help.

"Ahaana, I am going to get ready. Do you want to come upstairs and help me?" Jia said, as if on cue.

"Sure!" I said thankfully as we made our way to her room where the make-up artist was waiting. He was a real artist. He embellished her eyelids with a beautiful shade of turquoise that matched with the colour of her outfit. He stuck tiny little blue stones at the corners of her eyes, making Jia look splendid.

An hour later, Jia was all set to make Mr Rishabh's heart skip a beat, looking stunning, almost like a goddess. I could not wait to see the groom's reaction. As expected, the minute Jia stepped out in front of the family, there was a huge applause followed by shouts of glee that made Jia blush.

"Wow Jia," Krish said. "Rishabh better watch out. His heart might just skip a few beats with once glance at you."

"I hope not a few too many!" Saurabh filled in, making Jia eye him dangerously and making everyone burst into fits of laughter.

We arrived at the venue and my eye for details started taking in the uniqueness of the whole arrangement. The entrance to the venue was splendid in a very subtle manner. Orchids and white lilies made it look almost heavenly. A rain of light blue lights fell from every branch of the trees cornering the driveway. It looked like a princess's gateway! The guests that entered had appreciation spread all over their faces. Eager to meet the guy who had stolen my sister's heart, I followed Jia inside.

The minute Jia stepped in, the entire crowd stood staring at the new bride in awe and admiration. As we moved forward, the uncles and aunties and their comments came and went through our ears, making Jia stifle and smile.

As we neared the stage, I whispered in her ear, "Have you managed to find him yet?"

"No!" she said, barely looking up.

I poked her and teased, "Ahaa! *Sharmanaa* and all huh?"

"Shhh!" she said, shrugging off. As I looked up, I saw a handsome looking man drinking in Jia's beauty and I could guess the reason behind her shyness. Needless to say, it was Rishabh. I carefully escorted Jia towards him and smiled as they both looked into each other's eyes. In a matter of seconds, Jia's cheeks turned deep crimson, enhancing the effect of her make-up as she stood beside her fiancé.

Rishabh looked perfect standing beside her. The two made a gorgeous pair as they stole glances at each other like lovebirds.

"Rishabh, this is Ahaana, my cousin from Bangalore. I've already told you about her."

"Oh, yes! Of course I remember. Hi Ahaana, glad to meet you. Jia has talked a lot about you. You must know she is really fond of you."

"I am well aware of that Rishabh. I am glad to finally meet you. You guys make a fabulous pair!"

He smiled in response and I began to feel a little out of place, considering there were many waiting to congratulate them.

"Jia, Rishabh, I'll just excuse myself." Quietly nudging Jia, I made my way aside.

I wandered into the crowd of guests that filled the huge room, trying to find some familiar faces. Spotting my mother at a distance, I decided to join her. As I began walking towards her, my shoe-heel got caught on a nail in the carpet and broke, making me tumble forward. Lurching towards the ground, I shut my eyes, awaiting the impact of my fall, when suddenly, I got caught in a pair of strong arms, eventually halting me before I hit the ground. As I pulled myself together, I fumbled an inaudible apology, ashamed and writhing upon my callousness.

"I... I am so sorry," we both said simultaneously.

"I am sorry," I continued. "I did not see you coming."

"I am sorry myself. I was just looking in the other direction and stumped you in the process," he said in a gruff voice. He was tall, a little too tall if I could say, and good looking. But then his towering personality made me feel too small as I meekly tried to free myself from his still strong hold on my arms.

We both smiled at each other at the ludicrous situation.

"Hi, I am Soham. Rishabh's cousin!" he said putting his hand forward.

Taking his hand, I said, "Hi! I am Ahaana, Jia's cousin. And Soham is a nice name," I said.

"Thanks Ahaana." Soham grinned.

"Well then, it was nice meeting you. Enjoy yourself," I said.

"You too! Have fun and see you around!"

I nodded, walking towards my mother. I was both amused and embarrassed at the impetuous situation. I took off my broken pair of footwear and walked faster towards her, barefoot. I found her eyeing me in a peculiar way. Something told me that was not a good sign. I guess she had witnessed the little collision back there and speaking of my mother, who is ardently in search for a prospective groom for me, would be all ears, especially in a family wedding. Sighing, I tried holding on to an indifferent expression as I neared her.

"Are you all right sweetheart?" She stared at me with bright eyes, smiling mischievously.

It was so evident that that was not her concern at all. She was just trying to drag the other person into our conversation.

"I am fine, Ma! And please don't think any further about that," I cautioned her.

Not to encourage her any further on the topic, I excused myself to make a call to Ansh. I waited impatiently for him to answer the call before Mom could start with her suppressed ranting at my indifference.

"Hey Ahaana! How are you doing?"

"Hi Ansh! The engagement ceremony is going on in its complete glory. These guys have outdone themselves. I so want you to see it."

"Yes, I wish I was there. By the way, what makes you call? We are not in any crisis situation here!"

"On the contrary, Ansh, it is me who is in a crisis right now. You know how it is with Mom. She is literally on the verge of interviewing every good looking guy."

I heard him laughing at that. "I am sure aunty is a bit carried away with the situation, but she is not all that wrong, you know. I feel you should give it a thought now. You know what I mean?"

"Now you don't start!"

"C'mon Ahaana! We witness people settle all the time and it is beautiful. I'm not saying settle for just anybody, but at least give the idea of settling down a thought."

"Okay. I know the clock's ticking and all that."

"Yeah! Give it a try at least. Keep an open mind and tell your mom that you are okay with settling down. That itself will take a huge burden off her mind."

"Okay, I will explain it to her," I surrendered.

"Okay! You take care and congratulate Jia and Rishabh on my behalf."

"I will do that and thanks."

By the time I finished the call, my mother had wandered elsewhere. I searched through the crowd and spotted her talking to someone. She wore a big smile and there was a different gleam in her eyes as they met mine. *Now what's going on here*, I thought. As I reached them, I stopped at a good five feet when I realised the guy she was talking to was Soham!

Unbelievable, I muttered to myself, hoping to god that she hadn't said anything disastrous to him, yet! I pasted a fake smile on my face as I walked towards them.

"Ahaana, you have already met Soham!" She said as she caught hold of my arm and turned me towards him.

"Ah, yes Ma. I have met Mr Soham a while back." I tried making it as short and crisp as I could manage without being rude.

"Soham beta, this is Ahaana. She has finished her studies and has established an event management business in Bangalore. It is called The Threshold of Love."

"Ma, Mr Soham does not need to know what I do." I tried to sound as polite as I could, hinting, *'Enough, stop it here!'*

"It is all right. That is very nice to know!" Soham looked right at me. There was this weird naughtiness in his tone and it irritated me further.

I excused myself as politely as possible and pulled my mother aside.

"What are you doing Ma?"

"Arrey, what is the harm Ahaana? I don't understand. He seems to be a nice boy."

"I know. But that does not mean you have to give him my bio-data right now!"

"I am sorry," she said with feigned innocence, which nevertheless tugged at my heart, making me feel guilty at once for speaking with her like that.

"I am sorry Ma!" I said, slowly. "I am okay for getting settled, but just not this way, not so fast."

"Are you?" She eyed me curiously, waiting for my answer, completely ignoring the latter half of what I had said.

I hesitated before answering. "Yes, I am. But I don't want to go on a guy-hunting spree. I know you love me and want me to get married, but please don't start it this way, not like getting a burden off your shoulders. I will tell you who I want it to be with."

Oops! The minute I said that, she looked at me enquiringly and I immediately corrected myself. "Okay! You choose the person you like and I will see if he suits my temperament. Don't just show me off like that. I don't want to be taken Ma, I want to be loved, that too by a person who is willing to let me own his heart!"

"All right Ahaana, either you let me know if you have someone in mind or let us help you decide. And this guy we just met, what is his name, Soham. He seems to be a very nice guy. Radha Maasi was speaking a lot about him and I thought why not consider him. The family is good. And now since Jia is also going there, you won't feel lonely," she said all of this in a single breath.

"Okay, Ma. Right now, I don't have anybody on my mind. So if you really want me to think about this guy, give me some time."

"Take all the time you want, my baby."

With that, Mom gave me an excited hug, leaving me to think about how I was going to deal with this situation, let alone question how I managed to land myself into it!

Jia's engagement ceremony was the talk of our small social circle the next day. Mom and Dad had already discussed about talking to Soham's parents. It seemed as if the gods were against me, because Soham's parents had also agreed to let the two of us meet and decide for ourselves. Since we were to go back to Bangalore on Sunday, Dad planned to postpone our tickets. I found the whole idea bizarre, too fast an approach for such an important decision. But I knew it was better not to open my mouth.

It was Sunday morning and I was ready to go shopping with Jia. We were about to leave when Mom stopped me and said, "You can't go shopping today Ahaana! Jia please, make her understand. She is supposed to meet Soham for lunch today. If she goes now, she will be getting tired. Ask her to rest. That will help her look fresh when they meet."

"Oh, c'mon Ma! I am going and will directly meet him for lunch from there."

"What?" My mother almost screamed. "You can't be serious! And you definitely cannot go looking like this. Put on something more... more appropriate!"

Frustration began to build on my nerves. "Now what is wrong with these?" Denims, a red t-shirt and regular platforms were all right for me. Obviously I was not going to wear heels while I shopped.

"Wear something more Indian and ethnic, dear. It will look so bad if you are dressed like that!" *The hundred-year-old protocol of arranged marriages!*

"Ma, I am going to meet Soham, not his grandfather. And I am in no way dressed loudly. I think I am looking okay and if he has to like me, he must do so for what I am."

"*Uff!* No one can tell this girl anything. She always does whatever she wants to do." And with that she stormed off, still talking to herself.

I did not want to put up a show. I could not be fake. At least, not right now, when a huge part of my life depended on this. Yes adjustments are needed, but to change into someone else altogether is not fair.

I was certain about what I really wanted and didn't want to make a fuss about it. Sighing, I took Jia's hand and led her out on our way to have some fun.

As we sped towards the mall in the car, Jia was quiet and brooding. When I nudged her and teased her of thinking about Rishabh, she said, "I wish I had been more like you Ahaana, when Rishabh came to see me with his parents."

"Oh! Why that thought Jia?"

"Had I been as strong as you are, I wouldn't have had to compromise on a lot of things. Like for being who I am."

"And what makes you say that?" I was curious.

"Well, when they came to see me, I wore whatever I was told to wear, maintained as much elegance as I was told to, did everything I had never done before like serving them food and shying. That is not who I really am. I am the chirpy, happy go lucky type, but I was scared of showing my true self. And now, I am more scared that they would want the fake Jia rather than the real one. What if they want me to be all that I don't want myself to be?"

I thought for a while before replying because I didn't want to scare her. "There is still time Jia. I feel you must have a word with Rishabh about this. Tell him everything. But remember, where there is love, miracles do happen. Speak the truth and if he truly loves you, you don't have to lose yourself."

"Do you really think so?"

"Yes, I believe so! I have seen a lot of successful marriages, Jia. I guess love makes people want to do things they never thought were possible for them to do. I belive you two have this gift of love." Having said that, I smiled, being more than confident for my sister. I had met Rishabh and he was a great guy. And more importantly, he loved her with all his heart. He would surely keep her happy. And I... I still had to meet Soham and think about falling in love with him, if I we were to get married. *But planning to fall in love???* My heart screamed otherwise!

In Mumbai, shopping is inevitable. You just need to take one look at a store and you find something that you feel you just might need. We got so engrossed that I totally lost track of time. We were purchasing accessories when my phone rang. I absently took the call, not realising who the caller was.

"Hello?"

"Hi Ahaana! I am here at the restaurant. What time can I expect you here?" It was Soham! I suddenly remembered that I was supposed to meet him for lunch and he was already there. *Oh no!*

Jia guessed who the caller was and gave me an apologetic look.

Wait until Mom finds this out, I thought to myself. "Uh, hi Soham! I am so sorry to keep you waiting. I am stuck somewhere.

I will reach there in about... uh... ten minutes?" I looked at Jia for her approval of the time, for I had no clue how far the restaurant was from where we were. She nodded and we rushed out of the store and on our way to meet him.

It took us an impressive seven minutes to reach the place. Jia dropped me at the entrance of what looked like a posh hotel and wished me luck. Struggling to catch a breath, I gave her a quick hug and turned to walk inside.

I felt a little edgy and apprehensive. I had a lot of guy friends, yes, but having to meet someone for matrimonial purpose was a totally different ball game. I checked my reflection on the glass window of the restaurant and took in a deep breath, preparing myself. I walked towards the entrance, slowly and steadily, almost feeling like a brave soldier, ready to deal with life's biggest battle. If only the tiny fluttering of butterflies in my tummy would stop!

The beauty of the interiors helped in relaxing me a tad bit as it grabbed the attention of the event planner within me, taking my mind off matrimony and matters related to it. As I entered, someone from the staff, perhaps the manager, asked me if I had a reservation.

"I am Ahaana Agarwal. Mr Soham Sehgal is waiting at a table for me," I clarified.

"Yes. Miss Ahaana, this way please! Mr Sehgal has been waiting for you," he said as he led me towards one of the corner tables. Soham was sitting with his back towards us and thus did not notice our arrival.

"Mr Sehgal, Miss Agarwal is here," said the manager. Soham turned back immediately and stood up with a welcoming smile. I felt conscious at once and responded with a weak smile. He pulled out a chair for me and waited, a warm smile on his face. *Hmm... chivalry.*

It all felt so strange that I suddenly wished that I hadn't gotten myself into it. I looked at Soham. He was dressed casually himself.

He was handsome, rather very handsome, and then there was his smile! A genuine smile. I realized I hadn't spoken a word to him. Not even a 'Hi'. Feeling stupid, I looked at him and saw him staring at me with a funny smile spread right across his face.

"What?" I complained.

He stifled a laugh, making me shift uncomfortably, "Nothing, I was just waiting for you to come back here."

"Yes, I am here. Hi!"

He smiled back and said, "Hi!"

I didn't know how to start the conversation and he seemed to be of no help either. But at last he spoke.

"Ahaana, please stop being nervous. Consider me as a friend before you and I think beyond that. I am as alien to this as you seem to be right now. Let us first get to know each other better. Okay?"

His words literally lifted gallons of weight off my shoulders. I relaxed instantly and smiled back at him gratefully.

"Thank you Soham. I would definitely like that. Let us get to know each other first, right?"

"Right!" he said and smiled in return.

I let out a heavy breath. *This is so much better than what I had thought.*

We took some time to go through the menu and decided on the starters and the main course.

"So, how do you like Mumbai? Have you been here before or is this your first visit?" Soham said, beginning the conversation.

"I have been here many times. It has always been fun to visit Radha Maasi. As kids, we would wait for our vacations to begin and then we would come down to Mumbai and spend our holidays together," I said cheerfully, happy that I did not have to worry about any relationship puzzles at the moment.

"That is nice. I love this city as well!"

"Have you been here since childhood?"

"Yes, I was born and brought up here."

"Great!"

"I have also been to Bangalore many times. Work takes me there quite often."

"Is it? What do you do?"

"I am into the fashion industry. We supply fabrics to a major share of fashion brands pan India and are planning to expand to other countries as well," he explained.

"That is nice. I am sure work makes you travel a lot?"

"Yes, that is a part of my work. I keep moving around. But now, things are getting settled. I am staying in Mumbai most of the time."

"Nice! It sounds like work is all hectic and fun for you." I smiled.

"Oh yes, it is! And I think it is the same for you as well, right? Because I heard that you run an event management company?"

"Yes, that is right. My company is called The Threshold of Love!" I said proudly.

"Nice name! So you run it single-handedly?"

"No, it is a partnership firm. I run it with my college friend Ansh. We started it together."

"That's great!"

With some good food and light conversations, my meeting with Soham went well. He would surely make a good friend, but a husband? I needed more time to think.

Our interests, though not totally conflicting, were a little different. I liked indoor activities like reading or just a cup of coffee, popcorn and a movie. My outdoor activities involved mostly going on long drives. Soham, on the other hand, was more of a sports person. He loved games like cricket, squash, golf, etc.

"Well Ahaana, I think I like you as a person and I am sure our families would be going crazy out of curiosity to know about our decision. What do you think about this?"

He was way too frank about the matter, which was awkward, but it was also what was to be done practically, right? However, it seemed too soon to say anything. And where were all those sparks and funny things that people in love told me about? Those strange things that happen when you see the person made for you... Nothing strange was happening here. But then what was it that I was looking for?

"Umm Soham, I don't know what to tell them! It is just too soon to say anything. I mean, don't you think our staying in two different cities is a problem in itself?"

"In what way Ahaana? I don't understand!"

"Well, I mean, I have my company in Bangalore and you have your business here in Mumbai. I am really not prepared to shut down my business. And Ansh... our company is his earning too. I don't think I can shut it down."

"Hmm. I have a solution to that. You cannot shift your business here, but I can run mine from Bangalore."

"Huh?!" Now that was something I was not prepared for at all. I mean, men do take such desperate measures when they are madly in love with a girl. Well, at least that was what I had read in books and heard people say. But why was Soham prepared to leave his family and everything else behind and move to Bangalore? That made crazy doubts creep into me.

"Hey relax! I know what you must be thinking. The truth is my business has expanded quite a lot. Right now, we need someone to look after the Bangalore branch. We have two options. Either I go and handle business there or Rishabh shifts out. And now, since

Rishabh is planning to shift to the US, it leaves me to look after the Bangalore office. So, I thought, why not!"

He said all of this very clearly and with so much confidence that I felt things had been planned till the end by both families, and I was perhaps the only one so unsure. But with his saying that, my worries about him got a bit sorted. Now I had just one other major problem, which was, *did I want to marry him?*

"All right Soham. I think we both have had a clear chat. I like you too, but I need a little time before saying a yes. I hope that is all right with you?"

"Sure Ahaana, I am fine with it. You can have all the time in the world. But yes, can I say something?"

"Yes, sure." I was scared about what he might say now.

"I think I really like you. I am not expressive about my feelings and might take time to open up. But to make it easier for you to decide, I can assure you that I will keep you happy. In fact, I am confident about that. Till now I've spent all my time with my family and my work. I haven't been involved in any serious relationship. I have never had anyone before. But with you, I feel we can make it work."

I liked the way he said that. I felt that maybe this was how life was supposed to happen. *There were couples, rather many couples, who fell in love after marriage, right?*

"Thank you Soham. Mmm... I just have to discuss things with my parents." I told him, trying to keep the confusion out of my voice.

"Sure Ahaana!"

And then we both smiled. Life had left us to decide upon the most important matter of our lives. But I don't know why I didn't feel my heart supporting me in what I was thinking. Panic crept in again and I shrugged it off. It was time to get practical.

"May I drop you?" Soham asked me when we were leaving.

"Umm," I hesitated for a second, as it seemed too fast. But I said, "Okay... sh... sure!"

"Great! Let's go," he said enthusiastically.

We moved out and waited as his car came at the entrance of the restaurant. He held the door open for me.

"Thank you," I said.

He sat in the driver's seat. But instead of keying in the ignition, just sat, lost in some thought.

"What happened? Forgotten something?" I asked.

"Actually, I forgot to tell you. I had to meet a friend on my way back. I am really sorry, it just slipped out of my mind. Okay! I think I will drop you first, but just give me a moment. I will call him and inform him."

"Oh! Hang on. Please don't fret so much. I will get back on my own. It won't be a problem at all." I moved to open the door.

"Hey, no way. Stay, I will drop you. I insist, please."

"Umm...where is your friend's place? Is it on our way back or would you have to take a deviation?"

"It is on our way back. I just have to collect some papers from him."

"Well, if you just have to stop by, I don't have a problem waiting in the car."

"Are you sure?"

"Absolutely," I said smiling.

"Okay!" He smiled back and sped up.

We drove for another ten minutes until Soham stopped near a motel.

"Is he staying around here?" I asked him.

"No, he is just visiting Mumbai for some work. In fact, he is from Bangalore as well and is here for business." I nodded. "Will you wait here?"

"Sure."

I saw him go. I thought about being with him as his wife, sharing a life with him, the sound of my name if changed to 'Ahaana Sehgal'.

I checked the time and saw that it was going to be half past five. It was getting a little late. Mom would surely be biting her nails with anxiety by now. I helplessly kept looking at where Soham was standing as he waited for his friend.

Ronit

It had been almost two months since his life had showed him an unexpected turn. But Ronit had a vigour, which made him stand above all hardships that life offered. Even when he had lost his little brother Roshan to an accident, he stood like a pillar besides his family. Now when Taashi left him, he just decided to be faithful to life and not get provoked with the melancholy he faced. He had immersed himself into work, and right now, he was in Mumbai to procure some raw materials. He had a lot of friends here, but refused to see any of them.

But it was different with Soham. They had studied together in high school and had done their MBA together in the US. They had always been best friends. This time Soham had given him great news that there was a possibility of him moving to Bangalore and Ronit had gathered some information that would help him in the process. While he flipped through the pages of the book he was trying to read, he heard a knock at his door.

"Hey there buddy!" Ronit said as he opened the door. "Come on in!"

"Hey!" Soham entered and gave him a hug.

"It is so good to see you!"

"Same here, buddy!" Ronit stepped aside for Soham to get in, but he seemed reluctant. He turned towards the driveway and back again.

"What's the matter? Everything all right?"

"I am in a little hurry Ronit. There is someone waiting in the car," Soham said.

"Oh! Is that 'someone' the girl you went to see today?"

"Yes, and she needs to get home in time. I will have to rush back, bro."

"No problem. I have your papers ready. By the way, has my friend found the one?" Ronit winked at him.

"Aah, time will tell."

"Oh stop being diplomatic! Is she the one or not?"

Soham smiled at him and said, "I think she is."

"Awesome!" He literally squealed with delight. "In that case, can I meet her right now?"

"No dude. I am still awaiting her reply."

"Okay." He smiled at him and, after a pause, said, "I am glad you found the one buddy."

Soham knew what had happened with Ronit and felt a prick of guilt, but knew his friend better and thus smiled back at him.

"Thanks dude! Means a lot. Will see you tomorrow?"

"Hey, I will be leaving for Bangalore tomorrow evening. See if we can meet late in the evening today or tomorrow morning."

"Sure. In any case, I think I will be visiting Bangalore soon."

"I will be looking forward to that, Soham!"

With that, Ronit came out to see him off and squinted towards the car.

"Aah, it's too bright, I can't see her, but I am sure she is beautiful."

"She is." Soham smiled. "You will meet her soon, I promise."

Ahaana

I squinted as I looked towards where Soham was talking to his friend. The sun was too bright for me to see anything. As I listened to the soft music going on in his car, Soham walked back, lisping a sorry.

"Hey I am sorry! I hope that didn't take too long?" Soham said as he sat in the car.

"No problem. That was rather quick," I reassured.

I got a glimpse of his friend as he was waving back at our direction as Soham manuevered the car away. Although he was at quite a distance, somehow he looked rather familiar.

"Hey, what's your friend's name?"

Just as I asked him, the car came to a screeching halt. I was going to jerk forcefully towards the dashboard when Soham's hand prevented me from hitting. I looked up and saw a cycle in front of our car with a kid on it. "Gosh!"

"I am so sorry!" he said.

Frightened, I glanced towards the child who seemed really shaken. He somehow pulled himself together and with small steps, moved with his cycle to the other side of the road.

"Are you okay?" Soham asked loudly.

He nodded and gave a nervous smile.

"Kids!" he just said and looked at me. "Are *you* all right, Ahaana?"

"Yeah, I am fine. Thank god the kid is okay!" I managed to say, though I was a bit shaken myself.

"Yes! Thank god, no one is hurt," he said and we drove off silently.

The moment I reached home, I found Mom standing at the door waiting for me, obviously brimming with questions.

"Ahaana! You have taken so long. Why haven't you been answering any of my calls? Did you meet Soham? Is it a yes?" She laid out her volley of questions breathlessly, even before I could set foot inside.

A smile burst out at the corners of my mouth as I couldn't help but reel in the warmth of my mother's care. "Relax Ma! Can I first step in please? I will tell you everything."

"Okay! She moved aside allowing me some space to enter. The minute I got in, she began, "Now tell me what happened."

I smiled and moved in towards the sofa, kept my bag on the table and plopped into the beanbag nearby, aware of her frustration.

"I met him, Ma."

"Is Ahaana here?" Maasi came out of the kitchen, holding a spatula.

"Yes she is! And look at her Radha, she is not telling me anything," Mom said out aloud, with knitted brows.

Listening to all that chaos, Krish and Jia came out to see what Mom and Maasi were up to. Saurabh also came trotting behind them.

"What's all this screaming about?" Krish said looking at the three of us. "Give her a break, you guys. Why don't you wash your hands, get yourself some water and relax, Di?"

"Thank you!" I said, grinning at him gratefully.

Ma had no other option but to agree. "Okay! Go freshen up and come back fast. Stop taking advantage of the situation, Ahaana. And Krish, you go sit there quietly. Not a single word from you anymore."

My brother giggled and obeyed her, sitting down dramatically on the sofa.

"Stop teasing Maasi, Ahaana. Why don't you tell us what happened there with Soham?" Jia chimed in.

"Relax! We met, had lunch, had a brief talk and he dropped me back. That's all!" I said and started fidgeting with the remote control.

"Ahaana! Well, if you don't stop testing my patience, I shall call them and say it is a yes from your side," Mom blackmailed me.

"Okay!" And then after a pause and a sly smile, I dramatically said, "Tell them!"

The minute I said that, at first everyone became very quiet, very still. There was pin drop silence in the room, almost eerie. No one batted an eyelid. All of a sudden, it was my brother to break the silence.

"Yeaaaaa!" screamed Krish.

And then, suddenly, all of them screeched with glee at once, happiness broadcasted on all their faces.

"Ahaanaaaa!" screeched Mom.

"Yippieee!" cheered Jia.

Radha Maasi ran towards me and the next thing I knew, I was there somewhere between that warm but strong flow of emotions, hugged by all the hearts that loved me more than I could have imagined.

"Okay guys!" I said in order to quieten them. But who would listen to me? It was celebration time for them.

"Whew!" I released a sigh of relief as I saw five darling faces staring at me. I burst out laughing involuntarily, and stopped only when I saw Ma's eyes had moistened.

"Awwww Ma!" I went and hugged her. I decided then that I would 'go with the flow'! Mother's love emitted from every pore as I was engulfed in the peace and happiness that hug soaked me in.

"I am so happy, Ahaana! You don't know how long I have waited for this moment. Soham is the ideal match for you and I really like him. I am sure he will keep you very happy."

I simply hugged her again.

"Did I just hear that right?" Dad's voice came from behind as I turned to see his stunned expression.

I just nodded, as I turned towards him, nervous all of a sudden.

"Yes, our daughter has said a yes for marriage," Mom proudly offered.

"You did?" Dad looked at me again.

"Yes Papa! Ahaana has given the nod." Krish answered for me.

It was a different feeling when Krish told Dad about my consent. I felt shy, and then scared. *Had I decided it right? Had I done the right thing?* I looked at Dad for confirmation.

"Ahaana, now look at me," Dad held me by my shoulders. "Do you like Soham?" he asked. Now that's my father. The man I could count on to understand my feelings. I loved him dearly for this. He had always been my strength. And today, perhaps if he could read my mind, he would definitely see doubt in my eyes. He took me aside, barring others from the exclusive father-daughter conversation.

"Papa, I've met him just once and he seems like a nice guy. His words do not sound made up. But still, I don't want to be led by my heart. The heart muddles up things and leads you to a mess. So I think it would be better if you guys take the decision on my behalf. You know better what is best for me."

"The boy looks decent and practical to me, and affection grows on its own, in its own time." Even as he uttered these words, I could feel that he was trying his best to gauge my thoughts clearly.

"I like Soham, but I want *you* to be sure about him. This is about your life. You need to judge where your heart lies and then leave the rest to us," he added.

I nodded. "I don't want you to agree to get married only because you feel you are approaching the ideal age of marriage. Yes, that is one very important aspect, but then, I don't want you to make a hasty decision," Dad said.

"I get your point, Dad and I have a request to make. I would like to get engaged to Soham, but I want to have a courtship of at least five months. This would help me know him better." I cast a glance around the room. They were all looking at me and listening to every word that I said very carefully.

"Alright, I will have a talk with the Sehgals. But I'm not sure whether they will like the idea of a prolonged courtship," Dad sounded unsure.

"I don't think there is any need to worry about that. I think Soham will ask for that himself, since he said that he would be moving to Bangalore if he decided to get married to me and would need time."

"He will be shifting to Bangalore?" Mom asked excitedly.

"Yes Mom! That's one of the reasons why I accepted the proposal. I don't want to shut down our company."

"Wow sis! That will be great," Krish said fondly.

I smiled back at him and nodded.

"So, should I call Mr Sehgal?" Dad asked, looking at all of us with an excited eagerness.

"Yes!" They all said in chorus.

Ronit

"C'mon Soham, I have a deal to sign. I will have to get back, buddy. I just cannot postpone my flight. I am so sorry!"

"I am not listening to your excuses. For heaven's sake, dude, I am getting engaged and you've got to be there!" said Soham at the other end on the phone.

Ronit knew how important it was to attend Soham's engagement ceremony, but if he missed out on Monday's meeting, there would be a major loss for his company. He paced around his room. He thought of all the possible alternatives and then decided to ask his father to attend to the business meeting, just this once! It was not like he juggled his responsibilities often and while his father was a very busy man himself, he knew he would understand. Confident that it was a good idea, he sighed.

"All right, I will see what I can do," Ronit gave in.

"Do whatever you want, but just be there, all right?" Soham demanded with the authority of a best friend.

"Yeah!" Ronit couldn't help but smile.

"The engagement is in two days and tomorrow we will be having dinner with them. There I shall introduce you to my fiancé."

"What is her name?"

"Wait on Ronit. You shall meet her in person!" He teased.

"Hmm! So it seems that the sparks have begun to light, huh?"

"I don't know, but it seems like I do kind of uhh... like her. I mean I *really* like her."

"Wow. I see my friend is fumbling with words here. Such is her effect. This is good news, buddy." Ronit smiled to himself. "And, let me know if there is anything that you want me to do."

"Yeah! There are loads of things to be done. But don't worry, we can look into all of it tomorrow."

Saying that Ronit hung up and thought about what he could possibly say to convince his Dad, and more importantly, how would his Dad arrange that meeting into his tight work schedule.

But it was not as difficult as he had thought it would be to convince his Dad. "Don't worry son! Leave it to me. Go and have some fun. Convey my blessings to Soham," was all that his father said.

Ronit knew why there was this sudden change in his father. He understood that his father wanted him to have a good time.

Ronit had readily accepted his parents' choice for marrying Taashi. But after what had happened, his Dad's perspective had changed altogether. Since losing Roshan, Ronit's father had lost his zeal in life. But now, he seemed to be getting back to his true jolly self. *It must be me that he aims to focus on now, to alter my life.* Ronit smiled at the thought, sighing that one of the new missions for his father might just be to find him another bride!

Sunday mornings are so lazy, Ronit thought as he looked at the clock that hung on the wall. He decided it was not too late and so he had a quick shave and a shower before he set off to meet Soham. It was a ten-minute drive to the Sehgal residence. Ronit parked his car in the driveway and was about to approach the stairs when he heard Soham call out his name. He saw Soham standing at the balcony above, a wide grin spread across his face.

"You finally decided to come. I have been waiting all day."

"Relax bro. It is just eleven in the morning!"

"Whatever, come on in."

The door was unlocked and as Ronit stepped in, Soham was already there in the living room.

"Wow! That was fast. Someone is really excited."

"Yes! Keep teasing me and I shall pay back when it is your turn!" he said as he gave Ronit a friendly pat on his back.

They both had a quick breakfast and left for the designer's place to decide Soham's attire. It was finalised quickly, considering the lack of time. However, completing all the formalities took another hour. Tired, they decided to have their lunch at a cafe nearby.

Once done with their starters, Ronit called for the menu card again to place the order for the main course. While he pondered between the choices and ordered, Soham's phone beeped. His expression left no doubts about who the caller was. Ronit grinned as he folded the menu card and shifted forward, folding his hands on the table, all set to go on with his teasing.

"Go ahead! I am both deaf and dumb now."

"Oh shut up!" Soham wiped his fingers and took the call.

"Hey!" he answered as Ronit looked on with mischief evident in his eyes.

"Hi Soham! Is this the right time to talk? Are you busy?" said the caller on the phone as Soham tried his best to stay composed, ignoring Ronit's prying eyes.

"Yes, no! I mean, I can talk and I am not busy. Tell me."

Ronit shook as he tried to smother a hard laugh, giving Soham a hard time.

"Umm... Actually, I called to say that I wouldn't be able to make it for dinner tonight. There's some problem with my engagement outfit. I need to get it altered at the boutique and that will take some time and.... " After a small pause she added, "I am really sorry, Soham."

"No problem Ahaa...." Soham checked himself quickly from taking the name when he realized that Ronit was present there, with ears all perked up to take in as much information as he could.

Soham tried to be vague, and clearing his throat, he said, "Ah..hem *dear*...C...can I call you back?"

"Okay! Thanks. Bye!"

Disconnecting the call, Soham furiously glared back at Ronit who could not hold himself back any longer as he burst out laughing. "Dear?" Ronit mumbled between fits of laughter.

"I will kill you! I wonder what she must be thinking about me. It's all because you were listening to every word so intently that it made me nervous like a fool. Ugghhh!" Soham sighed as Ronit convulsed into an uncontrolled, hysterical laugher riot.

Ahaana

'Dear'?! Uggghhh. The word kept ringing in my ears, as if I had heard it for the first time. I was confused whether I had liked the endearment or not.

It sounded so weird! No one had ever addressed me like that. At least not really implying it that way. And today, there was this man, someone I barely knew and he had addressed me, not by my name, but by the word *dear!*

I was now getting engaged to that man. Someone who I did not know existed, not less than a couple of days ago. And now, he suddenly has the right to address me as 'dear'. *Uggggh!!*

Life was changing and god, it was changing dramatically. I wanted to clear my mind, steal some stability from somewhere. Everything was happening so fast. I needed to talk to someone to relax my fluttering heart. And there was none other than Ansh who would understand my situation. Taking my phone with a rush, I dialled his number. It then struck me that he had no clue about what was going on. But before I could hang up, he answered the call.

"Hey dear," came his happy voice.

Dear? Not again! That word! But it sounded so different when it came from Ansh. From him the word was just okay. He had always addressed me like that. But from Soham, who suddenly happened to have barged into my life, it felt as if he was crossing his set limit. I still took him to be an outsider. I was still trying to come to terms with the fact that I was going to marry someone I really didn't know. But...

"Hellooo, Ahaana. Are you there?" Ansh repeated.

"Oh... Hi Ansh!" I said with a deep sigh, suddenly aware of the phone in my hand.

"What is the matter? Hope everything is going fine there. When are you coming back?"

"I don't know. Okay listen, I will call you back." Confused and unable to concentrate, I was about to disconnect when Ansh stopped me.

"Hey, wait! What is wrong? Are you all right?"

"I don't know Ansh. A lot has happened here."

"Okay relax. Tell me what happened?"

"I am getting engaged."

"*What*?" he screamed so loud that I had to take the handset away from my ear.

"What the hell are you saying? Who the hell is the guy? When the hell did all this happen? And when the hell were you planning to tell us, once you got married? What the hell is going on, Ahaana?" I could tell that his surprise was gradually giving way to anger, making me giggle in spite of myself at the choice of his words. "What the hell?" he shouted again.

I immediately composed myself, reality hitting me hard on my face.

"I am sorry. I was about to tell you everything, but I didn't get the time. Now stop shouting at me and just get the earliest ticket to

Mumbai. I am not in a very happy mood either, okay. I am getting engaged, for god's sake, and that too when I am just not prepared for it," I told him.

"Who is the guy? I... I don't know... what does he do?" He took a deep breath as he composed himself. "Okay! Just tell me everything," he said struggling with words. His reaction was natural. He obviously hadn't expected this.

I heard him take a deep breath and wait silently. He was trying to make me feel relaxed, but I knew it was the other way round at the moment.

"I met him at Jia's engagement ceremony. My mom saw him, liked him and almost pushed me to go on a date with him. He seems to be a nice guy and now I'm getting engaged to him," I said, my words sounding hollow even to my ears.

"Okay, what is his name?"

"His name is Soham Sehgal."

"What does he do? What made you say yes to him? Or has something like love-at-first-sight attacked you?"

"No. Nothing like that has happened. There is something like practicality and age that has claimed me."

"So, is it an arranged marriage?"

"It is not yet a marriage, Ansh! It is an arranged engagement." His words were giving me the creeps.

Ansh let out a suppressed laugh at the other end. But soon he got serious and asked in a soft voice, "Do you like him, Ahaana?"

"Now that is the thing, Ansh. I liked him, but just five minutes back he addressed me as 'dear' when I called to inform him about changes in dinner plans, and now I hate him for saying that. I mean, we are not so close to each other yet that we can use such endearments."

Ansh laughed again. I knew he was by my side.

"Tell me, Ahaana, what does he do and what is he like? I want to talk to my smart, confident and clear-headed friend right now."

I relaxed at his words. "Okay Ansh. Soham is twenty-eight and into textiles business, somewhat related to the fashion industry too. He is planning to shift to Bangalore soon. My parents like him very much and my relatives support them. I met him once at a restaurant and he seems to be a genuine person. He is not haughty about his wealth and treats me well." After a small pause, I added, "Ansh, I am turning twenty-seven and the time to fall in love has lapsed. I think Soham is a nice person and because we both are here in Mumbai, we are getting engaged tomorrow, and may be, after a couple of months we shall get married too."

"Tomorrow? You are getting engaged *tomorrow*?" I heard a pause that started to bring in my worst fears back when he suddenly took off with high spirits and said loudly, "Great! We will be there tonight, Ahaana. And don't worry. Though everything is happening fast, whatever happens, happens for the best. Remember?" He paused again, as if waiting for his words to sink into my head, and for as much as I knew him, into his head as well.

He let out a sigh. "Ahaana, take care of yourself."

Ansh had already started thinking how to go about with the plans of reaching Mumbai before the next morning. He thought it would be better if Mishka was there too. He would help her out with unfinished work and they could leave in the evening. Speaking his thoughts out aloud, he added, "Mishka and I will catch the next flight to Mumbai and get there."

"Okay Ansh! I really need you guys here."

"We will see you in a couple of hours."

I smiled a little as he hung up, feeling much, much better.

Ansh called and confirmed that he and Mishka would arrive by 11.30 p.m. Thus it made no sense to hurry with my beautician and quite possibly hodgepodge my outfit. I finished at the boutique by ten. Grabbing a quick bite of a salad and a sandwich for dinner, I left for the airport to receive my friends. Krish had offered to go and receive them, but I insisted that I would go and pick them up myself. I had so much to talk about and had so little time left. I had to hurry.

It was not until 11.45 p.m. that I saw them walk out of the arrivals section. The expressions on their faces mirrored mine – fear, anxiety, bewilderment, all in one, making us all look like clueless freaks. But they had a touch of excitement and happiness that was left unmatched with mine.

I waited impatiently for them to walk their way out, staring into the direction they stood. As Ansh and Mishka neared me, they flashed their brightest smiles, being fully aware that I was currently the biggest nervous wreck they had ever come across. Before I could say anything, they embraced me in a tight hug until I felt both happy and breathless.

"Just look at you... you idiot!" Ansh said as he looked at me tenderly. "Have you eaten anything since afternoon?"

"Yes, I have," I managed to answer with a weak smile, glad that they were here.

"Ahaana! Oh my god. What is happening here? You're getting engaged tomorrow?" Mishka couldn't stop herself.

"Yes." I answered again and this time I was surprised at the weakness of my voice. Maybe I was too stressed and needed some rest. But how could I rest with such a restless mind?

"When are we meeting him?" Ansh asked gently.

"Tomorrow, maybe we can fix up a meeting in the morning, but then," I paused, "what is the point? The engagement ceremony is tomorrow in the evening. What can you do before that?" I reminded them.

Ansh looked worried all of a sudden. "Ahaana, I hope you know what you are doing?" Ansh said in a soft voice.

"Sweetie, I am sure he is a nice guy, don't worry. Ansh, please don't scare her. Ahaana is just nervous and that is why she seems to have doubts about everything," Mishka chimed in.

"Yes, I am feeling slightly edgy, guys. I am sorry. Let's just go home."

Ansh said nothing then, but just kept looking at me, trying to read my expressions. He had always been there with me, known me through our teenage years and way beyond. In the past twenty years, our friendship had been very special for both of us. And today, I know he really did not want me to do something stupid.

"I'll go get the car," I said and hurried towards the parking.

"I don't think she is ok!" Mishka looked up at Ansh as they both watched Ahaana go.

"That is needless to say Mish!... Maybe she is... I don't know just yet."

"Maybe you should talk to her tonight."

"That's exactly what I am here for. But I don't want to encroach beyond my limits."

"Oh c'mon Ansh! You of all the people have all the right to question her doubts and make her sure of herself."

"But when her parents have selected him for her, then I am sure he must be an amazing guy. I really shouldn't worry so much...." *I wouldn't have if this lady didn't behave so weirdly, so scared and baffled,* Ansh clarified to himself. He couldn't understand what was happening and he was getting impatient that his friend was not being herself at this major point of her life. As they waited, he saw Ahaana drive her way towards them.

He kept silent all the way as they drove to Ahaana's Maasi's residence. He listened silently to the conversations between Ahaana and Mishka, as she told her all about how she met Soham and how it all led to the engagement. Ansh caught the significance of how her mother had almost blackmailed about calling up the Sehgals and telling them that it was a 'yes' on her part and how she had casually told her to do so, until she realised what that meant. Or maybe she did feel the spark, but was unable to accept it right then. He hoped to god it was the latter. *Hasty! Un-thought! He failed to understand her right then.* But then again, he thought it would be better to first meet Soham before reaching towards any conclusion.

By the time we reached the house, it was almost one. We tried to quietly sneak into the apartment, not wanting to make the slightest of sounds that would wake up the others. I entered my room, only to find Krish spread on the beanbag, flipping through a magazine.

"Hey, you guys are here!" He looked up as we got in.

"Hey dude!" Ansh said softly, giving Krish a pat on his back.

"Hi Krishna!" Mishka smiled.

"What are you doing up so late?" I said once the exchange of greetings was over.

"I was waiting for you to get back," he said and his words made me smile.

"Thanks sweetheart, but I think you should go to bed now. It is already late."

"Yes di."

As he said that, I saw three very special people standing before me to share my life's important milestone. Loosing that little control over my heart that I had kept tucked in for so long, I wept, feeling the nervousness and all the 'un-surety' flow out in front of my brother and my friends in a rather helpless way. As if on cue, Krish came and held me tight followed by Ansh and Mishka, who engulfed me with worried expressions as they quietly let me cry.

After what seemed like an eternity, I felt better. Krish wiped my away tears and said, "Don't worry di, we will not let anything wrong happen to you, so trust what Mom and Dad have helped you decide. And listen, even if it is your decision at the end, it is not a bad one. Soham is a very nice guy. We like him, all of us do."

Once Ansh heard that from Krishna, he felt confident, but he did not know why Ahaana felt so devastated, so nervous. He had always seen the confident side of her. Always aware of what she was doing. If she was not in this with all her heart, then why was she here? He had to ask her that, before she did something that would hurt her and everyone else later. He waited patiently until Krish left. As Mishka got busy with her unpacking, he thought it was the right time to talk to Ahaana. He looked towards her, sitting by the window and looking out into the empty street below. She hadn't noticed that Ansh was still there, not until she heard him clear his throat.

"You didn't go to sleep yet, Ansh? Do you need something?"

"No. I don't need anything; all I want is to talk. So come, sit here," he said, patting the empty beanbag next to him.

Ahaana quietly obeyed him. He looked at her and his worry grew stronger that she was doing something that she was not sure about at all. He wanted to help her make up her mind. He was sure that had she followed her heart in this, she would have looked more confident.

He too had gone through such a phase recently. He understood that marriage cannot happen with an expectation that 'love' will happen later. It has to be felt and felt right! It is not possible to get married to someone for whom you feel nothing in your heart, however nice they might be. It was simply better to say 'no' than ruin lives.

"Do you like Soham?" Ansh asked me flatly.

I kept quiet for a moment and then met his eyes.

"Tell me Ahaana, it is just me here. Do you like the guy?"

"He is nice."

"That's not the answer to my question. Do you like him?" he stressed again.

"I don't know Ansh," I said getting irritated with where life had put me. "He is a very nice person, a gentleman in every manner. He is not self-conceited and he has a nice family. And... I will be able to stay in Bangalore," I said everything in one breath like I had memorised the reasons why I had accepted the relationship. I wondered if I was trying to convince myself.

"Okay, what are the other reasons?" Ansh said, after a brief silence.

"I am twenty-six and that is quite an appropriate age for marriage for girls in families like ours. All these years, I had been foolishly waiting for the magical feeling, which they always say happens when you see someone you are destined to be with. I don't think something like that is meant for me. I did not feel any such thing when I met Soham either. I still don't, if that's what you are asking.

"He is a sober person, well groomed. He knows what he is doing and is sure about what he wants. He has been very clear about his decision about settling down in Bangalore and he has clearly told me that he likes me. Now, I guess love will happen?"

Ansh smiled at me like I was back to being the little girl from school, back when our friendship began. We had shared a very special bonding, which was often misread by people. But we never felt the jittery feeling of love for each other and we respected that. We were blessed to have a friendship like ours. The way he looked at me right then, I knew he had figured that I did not love Soham.

"Ahaana, if you are doing this for your family, I just want to say that it is okay to live for yourself sometimes. It is your life that is hanging on the balance and any sort of compromise will eventually lead to a disaster. I know everyone wants this really badly, so do I, but then not at the cost of you. Everyone will definitely respect a sane decision now than see you hurt later. On the other hand, I do hope that Soham *is* the guy. You deserve all the happiness in the world and it is high time you find that someone. Maybe you're only really nervous!?"

I did not know what to say. I felt like crying.

"Ahaana, will you ever be able to love Soham for what he is when he is with you?" Ansh asked.

I had never given this a thought. This gave me a jolt that did not escape Ansh's keen, observant eye.

"Ansh, I... I don't know. I can't guarantee that right now. I really don't know what to do. I have given my consent but... I... Ansh, I am not sure why I did this. I guess I will have to go with this decision. Maybe later it will work out on its own?" My voice trailed off as I looked at him hopelessly, searching for some fortitude.

"Listen to me Ahaana, sometimes it is okay to worry, and when it is a decision like this, it is natural to get worried. But there is a difference when you are just nervous and when you are scared about a decision." He looked at me intently. "This is about your entire life, so think it over, think hard and see yourself living with him and then you decide if you see yourself smiling with him or compromising. The course of life depends upon the decisions that we take. We feel confident when we take the decision from our heart. And I honestly don't find that confidence in your voice.

"Your family loves you and will not want you to be sad... not now, not ever. It is not so late. It was just day before when you said yes, so to think that you would be jeopardised or cast aside by anyone if you gave a second thought, is stupid.

"Take a step that will be good for your life, a decision you are confident about. You still have time to judge. This judgement will save two hearts from being broken – yours and Soham's. It is not such a big deal that you are a girl and at the age of twenty-six! You are a great girl and you have a lot of guys mad over you. I would have also been one of them had I not known you better!"

"What do you mean?" I said, a hint of a smile finding its way on my lips.

"I mean, I know you are my friend, but I also know that your mind stops functioning at times." And he playfully winked at me.

"Whatever!" I managed to find my voice back as I smiled at this incredulous person before me, who had actually just come because he had heard the worry in my voice.

"Okay! Coming back to where we were, all I want to say is – don't go against your heart."

"Hmm..." I sat back and thought how my fears had suddenly vanished into thin air. Ansh had brought the fact on my face – the fact that I was not ready to get committed yet. Not to Soham! My sorrows seemed to hide away, my emotions out in the open, the reality of my heart dawned upon me. I was being so silly. I knew Soham was a nice guy, but I definitely did not feel that spark inside me. I needed to tell him that. Maybe he also had his reasons to say a yes. Hell, it had been just a day. He possibly could not have developed anything more than a crush here. What if he felt the same way as me? And if that is so, we both could come upon a decision of mutual step-back-and-think-it-over. Yes, both our families would surely support us. Rather, they would have no choice. I thought as a chuckle escaped me, making Ansh look at me with a worried smile.

I looked back at him with clear eyes reflecting a clear mind.

Ansh looked at me as I stared ahead and I knew he was aware that I was planning something.

"I can see the confident Ahaana back, but please don't be hasty in your decision, my warrior princess."

"But why?"

"Just trust me? I know you, so please give me some credit? Don't rush with matters. Let me meet Soham. It may be possible that he is the right guy for you, just that you are failing to realise that now. But still, I would ask you to follow your heart in whatever you do, not blindly be led by other thoughts and considerations."

"Okay! I will ask him if he can come for breakfast tomorrow."

"Fine. Now just relax and go to sleep. We will handle it together. God always has a plan. Just have faith. If this is what he wants, you will be happy; if it is otherwise, then you will find the guy who will keep you happy."

"Thank you Ansh!" I gave him a tight bear hug.

I smiled as he got up and walked to the room where Krish and Saurabh were sleeping soundly.

This was going to be a long night, I thought. As I waited for the next day to unfold, sleep was far from my mind...

Ronit

The breeze felt fresh as he walked. The stairs were wrapped in a plush carpet, soft under his shoes. He was dressed in a black dinner jacket and as he reached the landing of the plush dining area, he saw her, dressed in a white gown, waiting at a far end on the beach. She was looking out at the ocean. He recognised the place where they were. It was The Serenity Resort.

He took long strides towards her. And as he neared her, her back towards him, he wondered with all his heart if she would accept him. He knew he loved her, he felt it with all his heart. He placed his hands on her shoulder, feeling her warm up against his touch. Waiting anxiously for her to turn towards him, he felt her hold his hand. He turned to look at her face when instead of the waves, he heard a ringing sound. It was too loud and it made him want to cover his ears. He tried to focus on her, but then suddenly the ringing became louder, making him fall into an oblivion.

Ronit got up with a sudden jerk. Where was the beach? Damn! Who was the girl? He found himself lying on his bed. He strained to see the light on his cell phone blink, showing a missed call. His breathing was ragged as he sat up and brushed his hands through his hair. He reached out to take the phone lying on the side. It was two in the morning. *Who could've called at this hour*, he thought, as he looked at the display in the call log. *Soham? Lost his mind*, he grumbled to himself. *Must have dreamt of his fiancé and dialled my number instead!*

"Hi Ronit, I am so glad you called back. Am sorry to wake you up man, but it couldn't wait."

"If it's nothing important, I will surely kill you for ruining my sleep. I had been working late tonight!"

"C'mon man, I am very nervous. I am going to get engaged today and all of a sudden, everything is going to change. I need some clear thinking."

"Tomorrow buddy. You are getting engaged tomorrow! In the middle of the night, when the world is fast asleep, my friend needs me to clear his head crowded with weird ideas. Soham, relax and go to sleep. Sleep will give you a clear head. I will speak to you tomorrow. Okay?"

"Whatever! Just hang up."

"Yes. I shall do that if you don't in the next five seconds."

"Dude! What kind of a best man are you?"

"You're not getting married tomorrow. So, I am not the best man yet."

"Fine," he said in a fake angry note.

"On a serious note, just chill!"

"That is exactly where I am failing."

"What happened? The week knees happening?"

"I don't know what this is called. I am just so… losing it man."

"Listen, relax buddy! You have decided to marry her and you feel she is a great girl. Now it is a different thing that I don't even know what her name is or what she looks like, but I am sure she is nice. Yeah?"

"Stop mocking me! I need a friend right now, not a prick."

Sighing and now wide awake, Ronit propped himself up on his elbow. "Okay. Tell me what's bothering you so much?"

"It's just that I think we rushed into it."

"Rushed into what, Soham?" Ronit tried to be careful this time, for he knew Soham was serious.

"Rushed into this engagement! I mean, we have not really got a chance to know each other yet. I really don't know how she is taking the entire situation. I mean, I think we both need a clear head to make this decision."

"Has *she* mentioned anything about it to you?"

"No! Not yet, but am sure even she is not prepared for it."

"Hey…where is this heading?"

"I cannot express it in clear words. I am having too many thoughts welled up inside my head. To be honest, I'm not sure if I'm doing the right thing. I hope she is in agreement with what is going on. I mean, it is way too sudden."

"Well, if she has said a yes, then she must have taken it well buddy. So don't worry yourself with these thoughts. Let the matter take its course," Ronit tried to calm him down.

"No Ronit, you don't understand. I feel that I should've asked for some more time to decide."

"That does sound creepy now. You are not thinking of postponing the ceremony, are you?"

"Nah! Not that I can do so. That would not be the right thing to do."

"Soham, are you serious? What has gotten into your head? You are going to get engaged tomorrow. I cannot see any sense in what you are saying. You liked the girl and you said yes to her, isn't it?"

"Yes Ronit, I like the girl and I even agreed to get engaged to her. But this is a commitment of a lifetime and we hardly know each other. She needs to know every side of my personality. I must know if she will like both my positive and negative traits. What if she does not want someone like me?"

"So you are concerned about her to this extent?"

"Stop kidding Ronit! I am serious."

"All right, I'm sorry. What are you thinking of doing now?"

"I just want time. I don't know."

"Soham, I think you should call and talk to her. Just let her know what you are thinking. Make sure that both of you are sure of what you are doing. And if she too wants more time, then I guess nobody should have a problem with it. Nobody would want you guys to rush with the marriage, right?"

Ronit understood that Soham and the girl had planned to commit to a relationship without really knowing each other, let alone being in *love*. He did not want Soham to end up like him.

"Why don't you ask her to have lunch with you tomorrow? You both can discuss it then?"

"I was thinking of doing just that!"

"Just tell her exactly how you feel, exactly how you think."

"Yeah?"

"Yeah! Don't get nervous. You met her only three days ago and you are getting engaged on the fourth day. Don't you think it's too fast? It's quite natural that you are scared. People almost become a nervous wreck there. Just go talk to her," Ronit advised.

"Thanks buddy. I think I am that nervous wreck now, but you're right."

Ronit laughed, making Soham chuckle as well.

"Relax and go to bed! Meet her tomorrow and things will turn out to be the way they are meant to be."

As Ronit hung up, he just hoped that whatever was best for Soham happened. How could people take such decisions so hastily? Soham had never tried to understand subtle matters like these. But the girl, well... she seemed crazy enough as well to have rushed into such a commitment without fully knowing the guy, unless of course she had developed a liking for him. And that he could not be a judge of.

Sitting up, Ronit switched on the bedside lamp and took a sip of water. Just then, he remembered the dream, and the girl... He could not place her, but yes, she definitely was someone he knew.

Ahaana

It was six in the morning and I had not got any sleep. My eyes were drooping shut and I knew that the tiredness showed on my face. I had spent the entire night thinking on how I would delve my heart out before everyone, most of all, my mother. Just then, I heard a knock on my door.

Ahaana?

I heard Ansh whisper my name.

I sighed, relieved that it was him. I smiled in spite of myself as I got off my bed and tip-toed to open the door. Mishka and Jia were still fast asleep and I did not want to wake them up.

I peeked once again at them and stepped outside. The adventure and sheer secrecy of it all made me grin, for once, all the tension being taken off my shoulders.

As I sneaked out of my room, I found Ansh staring at me. Whether it was my smile or the fact that I looked like I was ready to conquer the world, I did not know, but then he too broke into a wide grin. His smile gave me the confidence it always did, making me believe that no problems lasted forever.

"I have decided what to do Ansh."

"And what is that?"

"Well…" I paused, "You already know. It is just that I don't know if what I am going to do it right or not. But I guess I cannot afford to let it happen so fast. I mean even if it is going to hurt a little, it is still better than me or Soham suffering in the long run, right?"

"Are you sure?" His question made me smile, giving me a fresh zeal altogether.

"You just had to be here Ansh, to help me think straight. I was just over-pressurized by my family and had begun to think that I was crossing the so-called 'right age for marriage'. I know that I have to settle down. But, I cannot do so blindly."

"Yeah!" He nodded.

"Maybe after some time, he does not like certain things about me and may not be able to accept them at all. Maybe I won't be able to adjust to certain things that might be really important to him. If we think through all of this now, we might not have to face all of *that* tomorrow!"

Ansh smiled. "Ahaana, if the two of you are meant to be, you will overcome all hurdles and compromise, but if your destiny is elsewhere, you do not have to do anything to meet it. It will come to you on its own. Just go with the flow. I will ensure that your family understands you and even if they don't, I will stand by you."

Tears of love sprang in my eyes, as I was speechless. "Thank you Ansh!" I stammered, holding back my tears. He simply held out his arms, making me calm down and bask in the safety of our friendship.

"Should I call Soham now?" I looked up at him as he let go.

"Ahaana, it is just seven. Wait for another hour and then call him. Okay?"

"Okay. I will tell Mom first then?"

"I think you should speak to your Dad first. In fact, your Dad and Krish both. And then the three of you can talk it out with your Mom?"

"Yeah! Mom might not understand it all. Okay, I will find Dad. You coming with me?"

"You want me to?"

"Yeah, I would like that."

"All right! Let's go."

And we both walked towards the balcony where my father was reading the morning newspaper, a hot cup of coffee in one hand.

"Hi Dad," I said.

Unaware of our presence, he looked up with a surprised expression that was soon taken over by a loving smile. I felt guilty at once, that maybe I was going to take that smile away. I looked back at Ansh who seemed to have read my thoughts.

"Good morning Uncle," Ansh began the conversation.

"Good morning Ansh! I hope your flight was on time last night? I am sorry, I had fallen asleep and could not greet you."

"No problem at all. I am glad you did not. I wouldn't have liked it had you stayed up late just for us," Ansh said with a smile. Nodding back at him and smiling, he turned to look at me.

"So my princess is set for her big day?" Dad said fondly, looking at me like I were the same six-year-old girl he used to pamper.

"Dad… yeah, I am!" I did not know how to start. I felt Ansh nudge me with his elbow. But somehow, I was at a loss for words.

"Uncle, Ahaana wants to say something to you," Ansh began for me.

Here goes all the 'I have got this now' and so much for strength and decision-making.

"Yes, tell me? What is it that the two of you are plotting anyway?" he kidded.

"Dad, Ansh was trying to tell you that… I mean I wanted to tell you that… I mean we wanted to say…" I was literally mumbling to myself and let out a sigh unable to shake away the nervousness. Dad eyed me curiously and patted the empty sofa by his side.

"Come here, sit and calm down." I did as I was told.

"Now tell me, what is troubling you?" he folded his paper, placed it away and looked at me, all ears. I glanced towards Ansh and then at my Dad and swallowed whatever I was going to say.

"Tell me?" Dad looked at me and then at Ansh, curiously.

"Dad, I am not ready for the engagement... the marriage with Soham," I blurted out.

"Nervous?" Dad asked sympathetically.

"No Dad, serious. I mean, all of it happened so fast that I just gave in to the thought that he was the right guy for me."

"So is he not? Have you heard something about him?" Dad was as patient as ever and right now, it was annoying. I did not know how to explain myself. Nevertheless, I still continued.

"No, I did not hear anything bad about him. He is a nice guy. But then, I am not getting that positive sign from within my heart. How do I explain? I know I am old enough and everything, but it has been just three days since I have met the guy and I don't know much about him, except some facts about what he does, where he is from and what he plans to do. I don't know what he is like, or how he would be with me, or how I would be when I am around him... there are just so many things I don't know. I just don't think I am prepared for this. Maybe if I get some more time to think it over?"

I had to give away all the options available; after all, it was about family reputations as well. I was really desperate that my father understood what I was implying. Dad looked at me and then gave me that tender, understanding smile, somehow just knowing how scared I was. "I was afraid you would come back to me with this doubt. That is why I stressed if you were in it whole-heartedly the other day," he said as he looked at me intently. I glanced away, scared that he might finally lose his temper at me and then, suddenly, he took me by surprise with his words.

"And now, I will have to deal with your mother and her sister." And then Dad smiled, almost taking the entire burden over, like my hero, like my saviour, like always.

"Thank you, Dad," I screeched and jumped into his lap, giving him a big hug.

He held me back tightly and then said, "Don't worry, it is better to solve this now than having my baby hurt later." His words warmed me from within as tears of gratefulness sprang in my eye.

"I was planning to talk to Soham, Dad. I will tell him what I feel and I am sure he will understand. You don't worry. We both will ask for some time to understand each other properly and then give our consent to this relationship. I am really sorry for being so naive, so stupid. I know I have put a lot at stake here, but I assure you no one will say anything, no unnecessary comments, I promise."

My father just looked at me and then said, "You have really grown up, haven't you. I know, it was all too hasty and I understand your mother can be a little compelling, but then that does not mean that we stake your life towards it. I will talk to the Sehgals. Leave it to me now."

"No Papa! Let me at least try. Maybe you would not have to go there at all?"

"Are you sure?" he looked at Ansh, as if taking his opinion in it as well.

"Yeah, I am!" I said looking at both of them. I had been thinking about what I was going to say to Soham. I knew all the preparations had been done. But since it had been just two days, not much was at stake, except for the two of us. I crossed my fingers, hoping that maybe he felt the same.

Just then I recalled he had addressed me as 'dear'. I recoiled at the thought that maybe he had already accepted things and was trying to make an effort. Just as I got into panic mode, I was jerked back to now at the sound of my phone. It was Soham! Uneasiness crept over me and my hands shivered as I took the call.

"Hi Ahaana!" Was that confusion I heard in his voice? *I hoped so.*

"Hey Soham! I was just thinking of calling you," I said in a careful tone.

"Yeah? What about?"

"Well, I was just thinking if you were free right now?"

"I am, tell me?"

"Umm... could you meet me for breakfast? There is something I need to talk to you about."

"Oh sure, in fact I had called to say just that." He hesitated for a second, making me feel more apprehensive about the whole thing, and continued. "I will see you in an hour's time at the cafe near your place? Would that be fine?"

"Yes sure! I will see you there." I hung up and looked at my Dad and Ansh, who were both staring back at me.

"Don't worry. I think I finally know what I am doing!" I said.

I took a quick shower and got ready to leave before Mom came looking for me. Dad looked at me hoping I knew what I was doing while Ansh looked back at me with a smile that said things would be okay. I relished that confidence and stepped out, preferring to walk to clear my thoughts.

It wasn't until five minutes after I reached the cafe that I spotted Soham. Immediately getting a grip, I steadied myself, preparing for what I had to say.

He saw me instantly and as he approached me, I could not help notice the distinct concern hidden behind his prominent smile.

"Hi," I said as I stood up to greet him.

"Hi Ahaana."

We both sat down and I tried my best to avoid any eye contact. The entire ambience seemed to get heavy as he coughed, trying to get my attention.

"Hey relax! I think I know what you have in mind," Soham said.

"You do?" I asked him, full of doubt.

"Yeah! I think we have gone too fast, right?"

I looked at him, amazed. My eyes were wide open to see how he had got that spot on. I couldn't somehow find my voice, so I simply nodded as I looked down, feeling more than embarrassed.

"Listen Ahaana, very frankly, I was tensed about the same thing last night. I mean, I understand that we have committed to each other rather too soon. And I also know that we can't claim to be in love with each other."

I was taken aback with his words, being exactly what I had in mind. The fear and relief, both were so sudden that I unknowingly left out a heavy sigh. I composed myself instantly, and gathering whatever confidence I had left, muttered a *sorry* under my breath. Unexpectedly, he smiled back at me.

"I am really glad that you said it Soham, because I have spent the entire night wondering what's going on."

"I totally understand Ahaana and I know it is too early. We both need some time to get to know one another, as friends first and then perhaps if we do find things right, we can take it forward?" He smiled and looked at me for an answer.

"Exactly! I would like that. I would like to get to know you first Soham."

Was that all? I thought as I waited. Something resembling the past fear crept back in. I looked up at him, trying to rewind his words and see if he had said them frankly or was it just so that it did not come out from me. I feared that my doubts might just be true and I asked him, "Soham, you haven't started liking me, have you?"

He looked at me blankly and then opened his mouth to say something, but then closed it shut again. I felt scared that after all I did hurt him.

"Ahaana, very frankly, things have happened very fast, so much that I really haven't got a chance to think straight, or for that matter feel the right thing. The day I bumped into you, I had found it difficult to take my eyes off you. And then when my family proposed to yours and vice-versa, I couldn't help but simply say yes. You seemed like the perfect 'girl next door' kind. But then, last night, when I was thinking that you might have your share of dreams and emotions that very frankly, I have no clue about, I got worried.

"I don't know if what I am would be what you want. You coming into the picture so suddenly, so perfectly in sync with my plans, I could not say no. But then, I thought it'd be better if we took out time to know each other first. I mean, I am not running anywhere, am I? And for that matter, you wouldn't either?" He suddenly looked at me with a grin, all the seriousness just vanishing into the thin air.

"Wow! Umm…" I cleared my throat and then began, "I really don't know what to say Soham. I am just grateful that you have understood everything without me having to say anything. I guess a thank you is all that I can manage right now. I feel the same and was on the edge, trying to figure out ways on how to convey them to you. I can actually never thank you enough for understanding me this way."

"You know what Ahaana, you don't need to say anything. We both were being really stupid to have agreed to get committed without even knowing each other well enough." He smiled.

"I just want to get to know you better and when I am more comfortable about us, I may like to think ahead," I replied, meaning what I said.

To that Soham smiled and said, "I will catch you up on that *dear!*" And with that we both laughed. This was so much better, so much easier, when I knew that he meant it only as a friend and nothing more. Not as of now at least.

"I don't know what's in store for us in future, but I would love to have you as my forever friend for sure!" Soham said, almost snatching my thoughts.

I blushed at being given so much credit. "I am just glad it was you with whom all this happened, else I wouldn't be smiling right now."

He smiled in return and then we decided to call our parents from the cafe itself to let them know that he and I had cancelled our engagement ceremony for the time being.

It took a lot of effort for us to convey our intentions to our parents, Mom being the toughest one to explain things to.

"What are you talking about? Stop talking nonsense and get home as soon as possible. You are getting engaged today," Mom said in an unsteady voice.

"Ma, please listen to me. I am with Soham right now and we both have decided to give it some more time," I pleaded.

"Ahaana, this is no time to kid around."

"Mom, I am not joking. I was stupid enough to do that earlier and I'm sorry. Right now, I know what I am saying. I want to be sure if he is the guy and only then can I commit to anything."

"This is absolutely obnoxious behaviour, Ahaana. What will everyone say? And what do you mean you need time? I got married to your father without even seeing his photo and saw his face on our wedding day. And you have met Soham, you had three whole days to decide and now you cannot just back out."

It was impossible to explain things to her.

"Mom, if the person is right, then it doesn't take even three minutes to decide. And if he is not meant for you, then whatever you do and how much ever you know him, time would still be insufficient to know him well enough," I tried getting philosophical, but it didn't work.

"Stop giving me these filmy dialogues. You are saying Soham is with you? I want to talk to him. Give him the phone."

"I will not do that Mom. It is my decision and his as well."

Soham heard that and offered to explain things to my mother. I nodded against it, rolling my eyes trying to tell him that my mother would never understand. With thoughts going haywire in my head, I did not realise that she had started sobbing. Her cries tore something inside me, as I felt guilty for being the cause of it. I bit my lip and then suddenly Soham took the phone from my hands.

"Aunty, Soham here."

He paused for a second and I was only hoping that Mom had stopped crying.

"Please Aunty, we are really sorry. I know how much it means to you. But, we are only asking for some time. We just want to know each other a little better so that later in future we both don't regret anything," he said it ever so charmingly.

He was quiet and listened intently, making me wonder what Mom was saying. And then he suddenly smiled and said, "Yes Aunty, I will make sure of that."

I looked at him with surprise.

"Bye Aunty and take care." And with that, he handed me my phone. I looked at the screen, but the call had ended. Just like that!

"What was that about? What did she say?"

"Nothing! I told her what you heard and she understood."

"You did not say anything different than what I had said. So what was it that caused such an impact on her that she agreed?"

"I guess it's a guy thing!" he said winking.

"I still don't get it. What did she say?"

"Nothing Ahaana, relax! I told her we needed time. Then she asked me if I was serious about you and would I give you the time you want and not leave you. And to that, I just said a yes!"

"What do you mean?" I asked him nervously.

"I mean that I do like you and, just like you, I want us to get some time to know ourselves when we are with each other. I want to give *you* some time to be sure of yourself."

I looked up at him and nodded.

"I hope the wait isn't too long," he said, staring at me in the eye.

I just stared back, unsure of what to say and what to expect from all that had happened in the last three days. I suddenly felt scared that I might really hurt someone. I did not want him to fall in love with me, not until I was sure of the whole thing.

"And don't worry, I am not forcing anything upon you," he said, as if he had read my mind.

I fell speechless once again and just nodded my head wondering what he meant.

"Shall we leave?" he asked me.

"Yeah," I said in a small voice. Why was I feeling so wrong, I couldn't get it. His kind words, his actions and his calmness made me feel like all this was happening because of me.

"Ahaana, we are friends. Please don't get worked up. We both need time, not just you. And we both shall use it to decide what we want from our lives. Meanwhile, I will be coming down to Bangalore this week. We could use that time to understand each other."

"Sure Soham. I don't mind that."

"All right then, shall I drop you home?"

"Okay!"

And with that, we left the cafe – me feeling a little less agonised and worried than what I had felt when I had walked in through the gates of that cafe.

I was nervous about getting home and facing everyone.

I wished this was some crazy nightmare that I could just laugh off and go handle some baby showers or weddings instead. I wanted to wake up, get deep into my work and not remember this gruesome nightmare at all.

I left out a heavy sigh and slowly walked in through the main door. The moment I stepped in, it was like an entire assembly of judiciaries sitting in front, waiting for me to enter and then pass their verdicts on me. I looked at Mom, who was looking really, really angry.

Radha Maasi and the entire family were looking at me like I had committed the biggest mistake of my life. I could not withstand looking at them any longer, so I simply looked at the other side where I met the compassionate eyes of my father, Krish, Ansh and Mishka. A feeling of security washed over me that instant and I knew that I had not wronged anyone. Yes, I had hurt Mom's feelings, but then it wasn't about just the wedding day or the wedding function. It was about my life after that and I could not go ahead if I were not sure of the person with whom I would share it. My family would understand – they would have to!

I nodded towards them and started walking towards my room. I heard Mom call me, but I ignored and shut the door. It was my decision and I would explain, but not this way, not in front of everybody. It would just be my family and nobody else!

Ronit

"All sorted?" Ronit asked Soham as he met him at his residence.

"Yup, I guess!" Soham had reached home and had to confront everyone. He did not like explaining things when he did not like what had happened. But he had to, so he told his parents. Neither of them showed any sort of anger, but it was his other relatives who he dreaded. They would start plunging into Ahaana and her family's character and go on with all possible nonsense one can think of. He hoped Rishabh would make his family understand things and not vent out anything at Jia.

"What are you thinking about?" Ronit asked, shaking him up.

"Nothing Ronit, I just hope my relatives don't pounce on Jia's family just because we cancelled our engagement."

"And why would they, what has Jia and her family got to do with it?"

"Oh you know how that old-age drama unfolds, don't you! I am the *ladka wala* and I obviously am superior and can just jump at any opportunity to point a finger at the *ladki wala*."

"Yeah? That still goes on? I thought that existed only in Bollywood movies and that too, the old ones. Even Bollywood finds that outdated now," Ronit said light-heartedly.

"Oh, you don't know! Well, I simply can't let it happen here."

"Maybe you could say that you both will get married but only after some time, when you are done with setting things up in Bangalore?"

"No dude! What if she doesn't like me at all?"

"Oh, so you are sure that you will say a yes to her?" Ronit asked, raising his eyebrows funnily.

Soham giggled at the look. "There goes your eyebrow stunt again! They always make this funny arch whenever you try to think hard."

"It plans to stay with me. There was this girl once that I had met in Bangalore. She was my wedding planner, when Taashi and I were supposed to get married. We were at Goa, finalising our wedding venue when my eyebrows played up again. Oh the way she had laughed! It was like I had got an extra face attached to me or something."

"Not bad!" Soham said eyeing his friend carefully. "You never told me about her? Was she a friend of yours?"

"Oh shut up! I just recalled it because it was pretty recent and you reminded me of it when you mocked at me."

"Recent? I think it has been well past four months buddy and talking of it, you did not flinch on thinking of Taashi, but smiled on thinking of that girl. Hmm!" Soham narrowed his eyes, trying to get words out from Ronit, a smile playing on his lips, conveniently forgetting about his own life's ordeals.

"Oh please Soham! Stop being a jerk. I haven't even seen her since then. Forget seeing, I haven't even spoken to her. And why are you trying to change the topic here? This was about you."

"Yeah whatever. I will not be the one saying no. I will get to know her and then say a yes!" He said being as frank as ever. "And now that I have confided in you, why don't you tell me about your wedding planner in a little more detail?" he chided.

"Don't bother going there, you will find nothing."

"At least give me her business details buddy. I might just get my wedding planned by her?"

"Yeah? In that case, I will give you all her contact details when you get down to Bangalore."

"Okay!" Soham had to give in.

"Listen, now that things are a little distant, I hope you won't mind me taking a flight back to Bangalore today? It would be perfect if I could catch up on my meeting," Ronit proposed.

"Of course. In fact, I will be visiting you soon, maybe within the coming week. And then, you could also introduce me to my future wedding planner once *my girl* here says yes to me," he winked.

"She surely will buddy! How can anyone say no to you?" Ronit smiled and gave his friend a hug.

Ahaana

"Thank god you booked the flight for today Ansh. I couldn't have stayed there for another minute," I said as the three of us were on our way towards the airport.

Ansh had made up an urgent contract for a wedding and took permission to leave for Bangalore right away. Dad had agreed while Mom was still giving me her silent treatment. I had requested Krish and Dad to try and convince her on my behalf, although I would do the needful once they got back the next day.

"Calm down. Everything is going to be okay." Ansh nudged me, like he had already guessed my thoughts.

We had three economy class tickets and had to rush to reach the airport with the flight scheduled for a take-off within an-hour-and-a-half.

As we reached the airport, we almost ran in towards the luggage check-in area and managed to be there right on time. We were the last ones in the queue as we went towards the departure area and hurried off into the aerobridge towards the flight. Suddenly an announcement took off loudly:

This is the last and final call requesting Mr Ronit Malhotra to proceed to the departure area for the flight IT 107 for Bangalore.

I halted abruptly, recalling the name that was buried deep in my mind somewhere. *Ronit Malhotra? In Mumbai?*

I looked around for any signs of him, but he was nowhere to be seen. Suddenly I felt Ansh tug at my arm. "Hurry up!"

As I placed my handbag in the overhead cabin, I couldn't help turn around expecting a glimpse of him, praying silently that he would enter, not realising that I was doing that at all.

Ronit

Ronit rushed inside the flight, glad that he had booked a seat in the executive class; the flight authorities had been a little more patient about waiting for him. He gave an apologetic look to the crew and took his seat after being helped with his bag. Looking out from the window to the ground getting smaller as they were lifted towards the sky, he remembered his small flight from Goa to Bangalore. Ahaana Agarwal, her infectious laughter, The Serenity and then he remembered his dream, with the girl in the white gown.

Feeling stupid about the comparison, he found himself shrugging at the thought and then, like there was something pricking on his back, he turned around to see if he knew anyone familiar. With no one obviously in sight, he just took a sip from his glass of apple juice, placed by the airhostess and promptly closed his eyes.

Ahaana

"Yumm...that smells good here!" Ansh came in with a bowl of popcorn in his hands, his nose high, sniffing the air.

"Heavenly is the word! First it is coffee and added to that – Ahaana special!" I grinned.

"I hope you are making some extra, else you won't be getting any of that," he said, pointing towards the cup in my hand.

"Yes, I am brewing some for you. I am pretty possessive over mine!" I chuckled. I was at his place, trying to gather some peace, and right now there was nowhere else I'd rather be.

"It is so good to be back! I was so far away from myself with all that happening over there," I said, sighing with relief.

Ansh sat back on the couch and handed over the bowl of popcorn. "I know! This was unexpected. But it is not over yet, huh? Now that you have some time to understand Soham, what do you think of him?"

"He is nice, but that's all. I do not really, you know, *think* about him. Though I know I've got to do that."

"Yeah! You seemed so lost yesterday. Especially while boarding the flight. It was like you thought he would come through the check-in area to you or something. The way you kept constantly looking there, as if silently praying that he did not come. Whatever got into you then? Don't be that nervous Ahaana. I am sure things will be fine."

"Oh, you got me totally wrong. I wasn't looking out for Soham. It was just that I had heard Ronit's name in the announcement."

"Ronit? Who Ronit? And what announcement?" He raised his eyebrows, tossing a questioning glance my way.

"Ronit Malhotra, remember?" I stared at him, wide-eyed, as if he had forgotten something really important.

"Ronit Malhotraaaaa….Oh! The broken-heart guy?" he said, looking surprised.

"Yes, whatever! *That* Ronit Malhotra." I said.

"Hmm… I did not notice the name. You have a sharp memory," he said, looking intently at me.

I did not notice the way he was watching me. I did not realise that my actions had spoken more about me than I even knew of. Ansh did not say anything just then. He simply smiled to himself.

"What is so funny?"

"Nothing my dear, nothing at all!" And with that he turned on the television, all the while smiling to himself.

"Hey Ahaana, tell me something. When is your next *date* with Soham?" Ansh asked after a minute or so.

I was busy blending the milk into my coffee mixture and replied loudly over the roaring of the blender, "It is not a *date*, but he is coming to Bangalore this week. I guess we will be catching up then."

"Nice! And when do you plan to get back to work?"

I had poured in the coffee and came up to hand over Ansh's mug, eyeing him curiously. "Who said anything about not being at work?"

"Don't you want to take the week off? You have been through quite a bit? Mishka and I can handle things without you."

"You are being ridiculous. I don't need an off. I will meet Soham if and when I am free. My work is not going to suffer because of that."

"Right! I get it." He took a sip from his coffee and savoured in the warmth he felt in his throat.

"Like it?" I asked him.

"Love it, thanks!"

We watched television, finished the popcorn and the coffee and then stood up to leave. As we shut the door behind us and walked towards my car, I passed the car keys to him.

"Is Mishka already there?" I asked him as I walked over to the other side of the car.

"Yes, she got there early today. We have a couple of events lined up. By the way, Rahul called."

"He did? What did he say?"

"He said he is in town and would love to meet up. He was sounding too excited for this to be a reunion." He chuckled. "I think he has some good news to share."

That's a lot of work, I thought as I looked at the number of events to be taken care of. There was an orientation function of a business house, a baby shower, a college fest and a couple of more events lined up. The orientation function was the first in line.

"Hey Mish, have you got a plan of action for the orientation?" I enquired as I sat back on my chair, stretching lazily, placing my hands behind my head.

"Yes Ahaana! In fact, I already finalised the venue with their team. We've got to decide upon the caterers and then there are a couple of bulletins that we will have to get printed for them which they want to be placed along with the decor."

"Okay! I will give a call to the caterers and get the quotes. Could you please ask Joshi to go meet the print guys?" I straightened up and began planning on what was to be done next.

"Yes, I have already sent him there to get the quotations and have also prepared a presentation that we can show the business house." Mishka beamed.

"Great work Mish!" I said smiling.

"Ahaana, there is a call for you," Ansh said from the other end.

"Who is it?" I asked as I reached my desk.

"Soham," he said with a wink.

"Yeah?" I said, simply taking the receiver.

"You want me to go?" he whispered trying his best to provoke me.

I just gave him a sharp look and took the call.

"Hey!"

"Hey Ahaana. Where is your mobile? I had to take the number of your office from your mother to reach you," Soham said.

"Oh sorry! And why did you have to reach me?" I asked with a sigh.

"I am gonna be in Bangalore tomorrow and thought we could catch up?"

"Already?" I said, before I realised. "I am sorry, I mean, how come?"

"Well, work! Umm... it is not a pressure though. I just thought you meant it when you said that you would like to know me better. Now we cannot really afford a lot of time for that, huh?"

I suddenly felt guilty and couldn't think of what to say. "Hey, sorry. I did not mean to be rude. It is just that with so many days off, we had a lot to take care of. That is why I was distracted. Sorry again, but I will definitely see you tomorrow."

"Oh? No problem, I totally understand. Great then! I look forward to seeing you."

"Yep, take care."

"You too."

And with that I hung up, sitting down on my chair, lost and staring hard at the ceiling.

Ansh was giving finishing touches to the presentation which was to be sent to the client for finalisation. He was way too engrossed in it and did not notice Mishka approach him.

"Hi Ansh," she said sheepishly.

"Oh hey! I am sorry I did not see you coming."

"Umm, I just wanted to talk to you about something. Eh... Er..." she hesitated and then gave in saying, "it's okay if you are busy. I will come back later."

"What's the matter? Tell me?" He said moving the laptop aside and bestowing all his attention at her.

"Actually it is about the business orientation event."

"What about it?" he asked, "Is there something wrong?"

"No! Actually it is on this Wednesday and I have some relatives coming over to my place. So I won't be able to take charge of the event that day," she said nervously.

"It's all right Mish. In fact, you deserve a break. You have become a workaholic these days. Go ahead and have some fun. Forget about this."

"Thank you so much Ansh! That means a lot."

"You are welcome," he replied smiling.

As Mishka moved over to her table, Ansh could not help notice the innocence that possessed those eyes, hidden behind those small glasses. The candid fervour and the way she carried herself, he realised, was something so rare. She was way too humble and right now, when she came over to speak to him, she looked so fragile. He smiled as he realised that he had never looked at her that way before.

It was almost eight and it was time to wind up, he thought. He took one last look at his presentation and then he shut it, turning off his laptop.

"You are leaving?" Ahaana called from her table.

"Yes, and I suppose you could too. It is closing time!"

"Oh, is it eight already? Mishka, are you done?" I glanced towards Mishka where she was leaning into her computer.

"Just another minute, I am sending these details to the client."

"Okay!"

"Ansh, I think even I will make a move. I am having a bit of a headache." She got up, gathering her things and walked towards Ansh's desk.

"No problem Ahaana. But how will you go? I had got you here, remember? Just wait for a minute and I will drop you," Ansh offered.

"That is all right. Krish is coming to pick me up. Just help close things here please and I will see you guys tomorrow?"

"Okay! Get back and rest," he said as I waved them a goodbye.

Ansh waited as he watched Mishka trying to wrap up things quickly. He saw her work nervously through her belongings and stuff everything in her shoulder bag that seemed to carry more weight than it could have been given credit for. He narrowed his eyes as he tried not to smile at the way she moved about at a frantic pace.

"Slow down there, you will fall," he screamed as he saw that she was about to trip over a small bin someone had placed right in the middle of the office. He walked over towards her and removed the bin out of the way mumbling, "I wonder who was stupid enough to leave it here."

Startled with the tone of his voice, Mishka stood still in her place.

"I...I am sorry," she said in a quivering voice.

"Why are you sorry? You could have fallen here."

"I just did not see it. I think Joshi left it here by mistake. Give to me, I will keep it over to the other corner."

"Easy Mish, I have it. And what's with all this nervousness? I hope everything is all right?"

I wish you would know, Mishka thought to herself. She couldn't fathom why he could not simply understand what lay within her heart, without her having to say anything. It was best to be optimistic about the whole thing. Realising she hadn't answered his question, she turned around, looking at him in the eye this time and said, "I am all right Ansh."

He looked at her in surprise, unable to understand what that was all about. He simply nodded as he walked behind her; he pulled down the shutter and locked it.

"Do you have your car?" he asked her.

"Nope, I travel by bus. I just have to walk down round that corner," she said pointing towards the bend, straight down the road.

"Can I drop you somewhere?"

She looked up at him, her eyes beseeching him to feel what was in her heart but suddenly stopped, feeling guilty and cheap. She was not desperate and if she loved this guy, she would wait for the right time.

"No, thank you. I usually wait for this little walk, it gives me some time to myself," she said, giving a small smile.

"Are you sure?"

"Yes, and thank you."

"Good night then and get back safe," he said smiling back at her.

"Thanks, see ya!" she said as she walked ahead, leaving Ansh looking back at her, unable to point out the effect she had on him.

Had it been any other day, he would have insisted on dropping her, but then today, with that look in her eyes, he really couldn't place it. But it had definitely made him uncomfortable.

Ahaana

It was a Tuesday afternoon. As I entered the welcoming premises of one of my favourite restaurants near my office with Soham, the air-conditioning within did little to make us forget the afternoon heat that we had just braved.

The fact that Soham had come over to Bangalore so soon was irking me, although I was not supposed to feel that way. I knew I had committed towards trying to know him better, but I couldn't help feeling that it had only been an excuse to completely get out of the situation. Feeling guilty at once, I tried to get rid of the irritation and be more in the present.

"So what brings you here so suddenly?" I asked as I took a spoonful of the biryani. I had to accept the fact that it was much more palatable than I had expected it to be.

"You, of course," Soham replied with a wink.

"C'mon, now that is categorised as flirting," I replied smiling.

"And what else do you think I'm doing, my *dear.*" His smirk had spread far on his cheeks now.

I simply exhaled and nodded; totally aware of what he was referring to, refraining to really push it any further.

"All right! I quit. I will stop putting you up on the spot," he said, throwing up his hands theatrically.

"Thank you," I said, finally smiling as I relaxed in my chair.

"Well, on a serious note, I came here for business. I was supposed to come down only later this week, but the clients here required me sooner. And once I got here, the work for today hardly took a couple of hours, so I thought why not convince the girl I dream of, to consider me a little more seriously?"

All that I could manage was a weak smile in response. I was tired of thinking about it over and over again. I wanted it to happen naturally to me, it could not be forced.

"I am sorry, am I getting overboard?" he asked suddenly wearing a serious expression on his face.

"Did I say something aloud?" I asked regretting that I might have.

"No, but I guess you must be totally bugged by now. I am sorry; it is just that I am nervous as well. I really don't want to spoil things, but I guess I start jabbering when I am solicitous."

"Hey I am sorry. I did not mean to offend you. It is just that the past week has been a little too much to handle and when I came down to Bangalore, I really thought I could take a break before I thought about all of this, I mean us, again. But I know I cannot take all the time in the world. I am the one who should be sorry."

"That's good! On that note, let us start afresh!" he said dramatically, making me giggle, as I nodded my head unbelievably.

"You really know how to jump from one mood to another, don't you?"

"Well, this is one of the many plus points of having me as a companion. This man here guarantees a long lasting smile." He went on.

"That he does," I agreed. "So what are your plans for tomorrow?"

"Tomorrow?" Soham said, turning on an austere demeanour, "I will be at this orientation programme conducted by my friend's business house and, unfortunately, that will go on until late in the evening."

"Really? Where would that be?"

"At some auditorium near Koramangala."

"Oh, I think that is the same one for which we are the event managers." I was surprised at the coincidence.

"Really? Wow... that is good news. I was loathing the fact that I wouldn't be able to meet you tomorrow. And you have organised it?"

"I am not sure of the name of our client because Ansh and Mishka have been handling that, but then, when you say that location, I am pretty sure it's the same one."

"In that case, I will get to see you tomorrow again?" he said, smiling broadly.

"I guess so!"

"Great! That will be fun."

"I don't think I will get to see much of you though, with all the work in hand."

"That doesn't matter, not as long as I get to see you."

The comment made me shift uncomfortably, as I pressed the fork onto my plate, trying to stab an innocent grain of rice.

"How was the lunch?" Ansh asked over phone while I sat on my bed, tired to the core.

"It was all right, we are still getting to know each other."

"That's nice. Well, tomorrow is going to be hectic. I will see you at around eight in the morning?"

"Okay then! You sound like you could use some rest. Sleep tight!"

As I hung up, I turned off the lights and in no time, drifted off to sleep.

I woke up with a start, only to realise that my alarm had gone off. I had a dreamless, sound sleep that I always longed for.

Stretching, I turned to look at my watch, only to realise that it was already 6.30. *Oh shit!* I jumped out of my bed in a hurry and went to take a quick shower. Thanking god that I had the mind to select my outfit the last night itself, I had little to do other than getting dressed.

I had chosen a maroon satin formal shirt paired with a knee length skirt that I loved and a black formal blazer. I adored formal attire and knew it brought out the best in me.

Done with dressing up, I quickly stepped into my black, brightly polished formal ballerinas, passing a brush through my shoulder-length hair. Dabbing some *Cool Water* perfume, I gave a final look at myself, nodding in appreciation at my reflection – feeling candour and confident! Work definitely uplifted my mood, I thought as I bid Mom goodbye, who by the way had managed to cut some slack for her girl. I smiled to myself, as I took my freshly serviced car out of the driveway, looking forward to a busy day.

I drove to the venue, reaching the auditorium in ten. I still had an hour in hand before the event began. Stepping out of my car, I walked towards the green room to find Ansh. He had mentioned that he would be waiting there for me.

I walked inside hurriedly as the morning chill raked through me. Once through the door, I welcomed the warmth of the place. Spotting Ansh at a distance, I walked towards him, amazed at the number of people already there. Dressed in formal suits, it was evident that they were all our client's office bearers.

Not bad! This company has a very punctual set of employees, I thought. I was happy to see that, since usually in such events, there would be a complete lack of concern by the people of the organisation. The event team could do whatever they intended and nobody would be there to question them. In fact, if my team was the kind, they could have easily walked away with just half the preparations and still go un-noticed.

Feeling enthusiastic, I observed how their employees took in every detail and tried matching it with what we had promised to offer. I had read the name of our client's company just the night before and remembered only a few details. I walked towards Ansh, who was busy reading a checklist and addressing Joshi. I was keen on knowing the details of this company, being so highly professional and organised that they appeared.

"Who is the main guy amongst these?" I asked him as he looked up, now done with his current task of addressing Joshi about where the stack of leaflets could be kept.

"That guy over there," Ansh said pointing towards a man standing in formal attire, but without a blazer, which I assumed would be worn later. "He is the manager of RMS and the owner is one Mr Deepak."

"Mr Deepak what?" I questioned, reminding him of his blunder. "You don't know the full name?"

He simply nodded and then added, "Give me a second, I will just find out."

"Don't be stupid," I said quickly as I grabbed hold of his arm just as he was about to ask one of the employees of that firm. "You obviously cannot ask them directly, they will wonder what kind of an event management company we run!"

"Yup, sorry! I am just too pre-occupied. Give me a minute, I will call up Mishka and find out."

We both waited as the call went on a no-reply. "Try again," I said as I saw a worried expression don his face.

"She is not answering," he said looking back at me. "Anyway, calm down! They are not here yet, and we have enough time. I will figure it out."

"Yeah, I think you are right. We are getting worked up unnecessarily," I smiled and said.

"Have you checked all the technicalities?" Ansh asked Joshi who walked past them, seeming a little too worried.

"Sir ji, err…" He was fumbling with words as he stopped before us and every time he did that, we knew something was up. Glancing back at him apprehensively, I stepped forward with a questioning glance, "What is wrong Joshi?"

"Madam ji, that projector is not working!" Those words let out a shout from both of us as we replied simultaneously, "Shit!"

"I will go check it out! You give a call to Chhabra Printers and ask them to send us another one immediately," Ansh directed me.

I nodded obediently as I dialled their number. I counted to ten as I waited for someone to answer the call. It went on a no reply and I constantly redialled with profuse hopelessness. Just then, my phone rang. It was Ansh! I took it immediately. "I cannot reach them; they are not answering the phone!"

"Calm down Ahaana, I fixed it!"

"What? Thank god!" I exhaled. "What had gone wrong?"

"There was a problem with the power outlet. You don't worry about the details now. I will be with you in a minute."

"I guess the guests have started coming," I replied, feeling slightly shaken.

"I will be right there."

The firm RMS belonged to a particular Mr Deepak Malhotra. Although the name did ring a bell in my head, I couldn't really pinpoint who it was.

"That name sounds pretty familiar, doesn't it?" I asked Ansh as he provided me with that information.

"Yeah, but I cannot place it."

"Ditto!"

We were waiting outside after giving our approval to the luncheon spread before us, as the guests would appear in no time. The earlier half of the event had taken off well and we were only certain that the other half would hold its grandeur likewise. It was when the crowd started pouring out of the main auditorium, that we saw their happy faces confirming our hopes.

Ansh and I were keeping an eye on the caterers when I saw Soham walk towards me with a wide grin spread across his face.

"Hi there! How are you this morning?" he asked brightly.

"Am good. How is the event going?" I replied with the same enthusiasm.

"It is great. After all, it is organised by you guys."

"Thanks!" I said sheepishly.

"I did not see you inside though? Were you waiting out all the while?"

"Yes, we weren't really needed in there, though we have a lot of work out here."

"I can see that! The food looks appetizing. Have you had your lunch?" he asked with a twinkle in his eyes.

"I will have it later. Thank you. Why don't you proceed?"

"Are you sure? I will have to eat alone then," he said pretending to sulk.

"I am sorry Soham. I really won't be able to join you right now. Professional reasons, you know. "

"I definitely do, just playing around. But get something fast in that little tummy of yours." He said staring deep into my eyes, which made me shift uncomfortably as Ansh smiled on.

"See you guys around," he said nodding towards Ansh. It was then that I realised that Ansh was meeting him for the first time and it had completely slipped my mind to introduce them to each other. Before I could say anything, Soham walked away into the crowd.

"I am so sorry, I am such a dork," I said looking at him delinquently.

"Breathe easy dear. I will meet him again. He doesn't seem so bad!" he said, raising an eyebrow.

"Yeah? I will keep that in mind," I said looking away.

"Okay, I will go take a look at the tables."

"Sure, I will go check if things are okay inside," I said and we both walked into different directions.

Just then, my phone vibrated. It was Krish.

"Hi Ahaana, I am sorry to call in between your event, but I really need a favour."

"What happened? Is everything all right?"

"Yeah yeah, everything is fine. Listen, I really need your car today. I was going to take Dad's, but he said he needs it. Since you are going to be at the auditorium the entire day today and not really travelling about, can I *pleeeeaase* take it?"

I sighed, comprehending the possibility of needing it, but thought otherwise and decided that I would be here well until late in the evening. "Okay! You can have it," I replied smiling.

"Oh thank you. I will come back with it before six!"

"No problem Krish! I will ask Ansh to drop me back. You can have it. I will leave the keys with Joshi; just ring him up and take it," I offered.

"Will do that. Thanks and love ya."

"Me too!" I said as I smiled fondly.

Hanging up, I walked ahead finding my way amongst the gathering. As I sauntered inside, I realised that there was very little light. What emitted from the podium was all that was there to light the area around. I wondered what was going on as I tip-toed carefully, finding my way over the carpeted staircase on the side of the seating. I tried searching for my team members when I felt a tap on my shoulders. I turned around with a start to find a man clad in a business suit, but could not really make out his face, which was hidden in the darkness.

"Excuse me miss, are you one of the members of the event management team?" he said in a *very* familiar voice.

"Eh... yes sir," I hesitated and I did not know why.

"There seems to be some problem with the lights here, as you can see. Could you please get this sorted out?" His demeanour was very polite which made me wonder if he was *the* Mr Deepak Malhotra.

"I am really sorry, sir, there must be some technical error. I will get this resolved within a minute." I turned around to leave when he added, "Also it would be great if you could arrange for a spare mic?" he asked gently.

"Sure sir," I said turning back and as I was about to step down towards the green room, the auditorium suddenly lit up with bright lights emanating from all the right corners. I whirled around immediately to acknowledge the fact, "Sir, it's bac..." but was suddenly at a loss of words as I stared back at man standing before me.

Ronit Malhotra! My mind screamed, as I stood grounded, my eyes fixated on his familiar face. *Doubt, question, surprise, happiness;* all the expressions that could be managed, mirrored in both our eyes at the same time.

"You've got to be kidding me," I said under my breath as I felt my stomach do a funny flip-flop.

"Ahaana? Hi!" He stared back as a smile lightened up his handsome face.

Not bad! He remembers me, I thought, not knowing why his sudden reappearance squeezed out all the air from my lungs.

"Hi Ronit!" I could barely find my voice as I gazed at his perfect features, confusion and familiarity dancing in his eyes as he stared back at me. For a minute, we stood still, neither of us making an attempt to move, nor say anything, but simply looking at each other. I did not understand why my heart was pounding the way it was.

"I didn't know this was your company," I offered trying to maintain all the reserve I could manage, to not run away from those eyes.

"Yes, RMS is my company!" he replied without shifting his gaze.

"Of course," I stammered. That explained why the name Mr Deepak Malhotra sounded so familiar; that was his father. *If only I had researched my facts earlier, I wouldn't really have been in this spot,* I grumbled to myself.

Yeah right! Like you'd still have the nerves, a small voice came from within as I scowled at myself for being so naive.

"I did not know you guys were our event managers, else I would have come and greeted you much earlier," he replied speaking my mind out loud.

"Same here." I didn't know what had got into me. *Where was my set of vocabulary and where was my voice?*

"So how are you doing, Ahaana?"

"I am doing good. How are you Ronit?"

"I am doing good as well. Thank you!"

"Umm, I'd better go get you your spare mic before the guests come back."

"Oh, yes please! Thank you once again."

"No problem at all. Ummm.... I will see you around?"

"Sure."

He looked at me with a questioning glance, like he was waiting to know if I had something more to add.

"Uhh... okay, bye!" I said immediately, as he smiled and gave way for me to move out. I managed to squeeze past him and without having the nerve to turn back, I sprinted out of the hall. The minute I was out through the huge gates, I sucked in a deep breath, trying my best to get a grip over myself.

"Ahaana! Where were you?" I jumped at the sound of Ansh's voice.

"Ahaana? What's the matter?"

"Nothing Ansh! Uh... they require a spare mic inside, could you please send for one?" I managed to say.

"Okay! But you stay here, you seriously look funny."

"I am fine, really. Don't worry." I managed as he rushed towards the green room and then disappeared leaving me alone, engulfed in a series of unknown emotions.

As I stood there, a part of me wanted to go back inside and talk to him. To ask him how he had been, which was the most natural thing that anyone did when they met someone they knew. But then, there was another part of me that stopped me right there.

I did not like the sound of my heartbeat and did not want to fathom any weird ideas that I might have developed a crush on that guy. Not now, not when I was supposed to try to know someone else. And yes, crushes were for little girls, right? I thought better of it and stood there, not moving a muscle, not thinking of anyone or anything, just waiting for the time when I could go back home.

Ronit

As he had watched Ahaana walking out at an unbelievable speed, in spite of those high-heeled shoes that she wore, Ronit could not take his eyes off her. And even now, as she stood behind those closed glass doors, something altered within him. The beating in his heart was never as prominent as it was right then and he felt his fingers moisten inside his pockets.

He remembered thinking about her on his flight back from Mumbai. He recollected the way she had become a good friend, the kind with whom he had shared his heart out. He had even let her in, onto the memories of his brother. But then, they had drifted apart.

After Taashi broke up with him, the last interaction between them was when he had called to inform her about his situation.

And today, now, when she had stood before him, so suddenly, he could not take his eyes off her. Her hazel eyes held his and he had wanted that to last… a little longer than it had.

Right then, he was willing to walk out to where she stood with her back at him. He wanted to know how she had been. He wanted to just talk to her, hear her voice.

What he felt right then was something that he had never experienced before. Ronit was used to being in control and control was exactly what he was lacking. And *that* made him very uncomfortable.

Ronit shifted his weight from one foot to another as he tried to ignore the thumping in his chest. He had business to deal with and he could not let his mind get confused at this very minute. He removed his glasses and rubbed a hand over his face. Brushing his hair with his fingers, he wore them on again. Wearing back his serious expression, he walked ahead to take over the event.

Ahaana

It was almost six and the orientation programme had gotten over half an hour ago. Soham had called while he was leaving almost two hours ago, asking if I could leave with him. Work had obviously not provided me with the spare time and I had had to refuse the invitation. I requested him to cancel the dinner as well as I already felt very tired. Thankfully, he did not press and had left.

I finished getting the bulletins removed while Ansh got the props and technical items loaded into the van. In an unconscious attempt, I looked around for Ronit, but found no sight of him. Shaking away the anxiety I felt, I groaned, unsure about the directions of my thoughts. *What has gotten into me?* Shrugging, I looked at where Ansh was standing, engrossed in making sure everything was done right. From the looks of it, he was going to stay longer.

I checked my watch and it was almost past seven. Added to it, my migraine was getting unbearable with every passing minute. Suddenly, there was a loud thud as one of the LCD screen boards screeched as it slipped from the hands of the workers.

"Be careful, Mr Joshi," Ansh called out as the group of men managed to save it from damage.

I could not obviously leave him to do everything on his own and so, I decided to stay.

"Ahaana." Ansh called out swaying his arms. "Come here!"

Exhausted, I walked down with a blank expression and looked up at him upon reaching his side.

"Listen, I think this is going to take a while. Do you want me to drop you home first?"

My ever-so-thoughtful friend! I thought and smiled weakly. "I will stay. We can go when everything is done."

"Don't be stupid. I wouldn't want you to deal with the labourers here and it's getting dark."

Tired as I was, I agreed. "Okay, I will go, but I will hail a cab."
He gave me an unsure look.

"Cabs are safe, Ansh!" I said rolling my eyes. "Plus, it is not more than a half an hour's drive from here."

"Okay, I will book one for you," he said as he took out his phone and opened the app to book. I waited as he finished.

"It is done. He will be here in five minutes."

"Okay, I will wait around and leave when it arrives."

"Are you sure?"

"Absolutely!"

"Okay, give me a call when you leave and once you reach. Okay?" Ansh almost commanded.

"Will do! Now you move," I said trying to push him with both my hands. He smiled as he wandered back inside the auditorium.

Fifteen minutes had passed and there was still no cab in sight. I thought of calling Ansh and took out my phone to dial his number.

"Hi Ahaana!" Listening to the familiar voice, I spun around, my heartbeat getting faster within seconds.

"Hi!" I squeaked, not recognising the sound of my own voice.

"Waiting for someone?" Ronit stood straight, holding his blazer hung roughly over one broad shoulder. The tie he wore earlier was absent from its place and the top two buttons of his shirt were tiredly undone, revealing a shy display of his chest hair.

I swallowed as I replied feeling foolish, "Yes, my cab is going to be here any moment."

"I see!" Either he was aware of the effect he was having on me and was teasing, enjoying to his benefit, or it was plain unintentional that he added that unbelievably handsome smile to that cherubic, yet manly face. I felt at a loss of words all over again and waited for him to oblige instead. He shifted his weight from one foot to another as he spoke, "Where are you heading to?"

"Home," I said, finding it an obvious answer.

"May I drop you?" he suggested.

"Hey, that is really not required. I wouldn't want to take your time. Thank you though," I said as I dug my heels into the ground ignorantly.

"All right, I won't press if that makes you uncomfortable."

"Oh, it is not that at all. Really," I said regretting my words immediately.

"No problem," he said. "Take care and hope to see you again."

"Yeah sure. Thanks."

As he left, I closed my eyes, not wanting to open them ever. I waited impatiently for another five minutes and then decided to take an auto-rickshaw instead. As I walked outside the gate, along the high walls of the auditorium, I realised it was quite dark and felt a little unsure of what I was doing.

"Having second thoughts? I don't think it is a good idea to walk alone at this hour!" Taken aback, I whirled around and saw Ronit, standing by a black car I had just walked past.

"Do you have to freak me out every time I see you?" I said, overwhelmed.

"I am sorry. But really, looking at you look like this, I don't think it would be a good idea," he said pointing towards a group of men, shrewdly dressed, standing near an auto stand, looking in my direction. I hesitated and looked up at him, grateful that he was here, in spite of the goosebumps on my arms, caused by his presence.

He opened the left front door of his car, silently offering me to get in, to which I obeyed without saying another word. Softly closing the door as I sat inside, he walked over to the other side and got into the driver's seat. I looked down, fidgeting with my purse, waiting for him to key in the ignition.

Ronit

Driving silently, they both wondered how to break the ice. Ronit felt different, he felt happy seeing her again and as he saw her, looking straight ahead at the road, clasping her hands together, he smiled to himself. He wondered what she might be thinking, given the fact that he had not bothered to call her again after so curtly withdrawing from a confirmed deal. It wasn't really the deal though; she had become a good friend back then. What would she be thinking of him – some spoilt rich guy, with an ego as big as his bank account? He flinched at the thought as he stole a glance towards her while she continued to stare at the road ahead.

Ahaana

I could feel his gaze on me as I fumbled with my fingers. I felt awkward and nothing came to my mind. I hadn't even bothered to ask him if he had been all right since his break-up. Being a friend, that much was obviously expected out of me. No wonder he had been so utterly formal earlier.

Almost on impulse, I looked up at him.

"I... I am sorry," we both muttered at the same instant and surprised with that sudden exchange, we stared at one another with raised eyebrows.

"Oh! Well... sorry," I croaked.

There was a long pause and the way he was scrutinizing me, I had no clue about what to do with myself. Ronit cleared his throat, wearing a penetrative look in his eyes and said something inaudible.

"I am sorry?" I asked again, giving him a clueless look.

"Well," he said, running a hand over his head, "You didn't hear?"

He paused, as if to take in my expressions. "Are you not going to say anything?" He questioned, still looking at me.

"Umm, no... Not to..." I hesitated, swallowing.

"Not to embarrass me?"

"Umm....Yeah... Some cousin of that."

Ronit arched his eyebrows, twitched his lips and nodded towards me.

I looked down at my fingers as they clutched at the hem of my skirt.

Ronit cleared his throat and stifled a cough, staring back at me, making me shift uncomfortably in my seat. "I am sorry, Ahaana, but I think I definitely owe you an apology," he began.

"Apologise? What for? It is me who needs to say sorry here," I replied, unable to understand what made him say that.

"For wasting your time the... umm... last time!" he said looking ahead.

"I don't understand."

"Well.... about just cancelling the deal over my wedding so abruptly. I did not even thank you well enough for the efforts you guys put in. And talking about the contempt you must have had to go through to back out on the appointments you had made for me... it's just, I really am sorry."

I stared at his eyes which looked right into mine, meaning every word that he had said. The compassion and the intensity of that gaze sent a shiver down my spine, making the words that I was about to say, choke up into my throat.

"Oh please! That wasn't your fault." I meant it. "Nothing could measure up the hurt that you must have felt," I added, only to realise a split second later that I might be getting personal.

"Thank you. That makes me feel better." He exhaled. "I guess it was the guilt and everything else mixed up together that I couldn't muster up the courage to call you back." I was quiet. "We did become good friends," he said. It was as if he could look right through me, making me look away immediately. "I should have done a little more than just call you and withdraw."

"You did the right thing the right way, Ronit. You did not welsh in any manner that you think of. You had hired us for your marriage and when that did not happen, you calling us to inform was the most that was expected from you and you did that. Instead, when you mention, that we had become friends, it was I who should have called to check on you. Hence, I am the one who should be apologising here and not you."

"Well! In that case… that makes two of us and now that you have forgiven me so generously, I say the same!" Winking at me, Ronit drove ahead.

A grin escaped as I felt a little more comfortable.

"Treat this as an off-track comment, but you are looking very beautiful tonight," he suddenly said.

"Well okay. Thanks and I will pretend I did not hear that." *Jeez.* I blushed, in spite of myself.

"Today's event was very well organised. Thank you," Ronit said getting some casualness in his tone.

"Thank you! "

"Yeah, we liked it and our guests liked it as well. You will have quite a few offers in queue for more such events that our clients organise."

"Oh that's great. We are grateful to you!"

"No need of that. Good calibre talks for itself."

I smiled looking at him, which he returned with one that caught a heartbeat within me.

As we neared my house, I asked him to stop.

He braked and I looked at him. "Okay, so we're home!" I said.

He nodded.

"So I will see you around?"

"Yup! Will see you around."

I lingered for another minute and then pursing my lips, moved to open the door.

"Allow me," he said as he got off swiftly and reached my side in no time to open the door for me.

"Thank you," I said as I got off.

"Anytime! Take care, Ahaana! It was nice to meet you again."

"Same here Ronit. Take care."

We stood together, staring silently at each other. He was standing a little too close as I shifted uncomfortably and moved a step back. He realised he was standing in my way and backed up immediately. He shoved his hands in his pockets, looking down sheepishly.

"Sorry," he said slowly.

I looked up at him and said, "Good night" with a small smile as I walked towards the entrance of my house. I looked back and saw him standing there, looking at me, with his hands still in his pockets, his shoulders squared, looking at me with his lips curling up at the corners of his mouth in a faint smile.

"Bye," I called out softly as he waved back and rode away. Smiling in spite of myself, I walked inside, towards my room and closed the door behind me. I had not expected it to be this way. Why was *all that* fluttering happening within me and why was I not in control of myself, this I could not fathom. It was almost barbaric and I tried to gather myself.

I took off my shoes and collapsed onto my bed, too tired to change, way more exhausted than I actually felt.

I was lost in my thoughts when my phone vibrated abruptly. Looking at the screen I saw Ansh's face flash back at me.

"Hi!" I said lazily.

"Hi, you did not call upon reaching. All okay?"

"Yes! Everything is all right. I am just tired, that's all."

"Okay then. I will see you tomorrow?"

"All right. Tomorrow."

"Bye then. Good night."

"Good night, Ansh."

If he heard the unusual ring in my voice, he made no mention of it. I walked towards my dressing mirror and studied my reflection.

Treat this as an off-track comment, but you are looking very beautiful tonight, Ronit's words hung in my head. I looked at myself, as the colour crimson reflected on my cheeks. Smiling at my reflection, I tried imitating his tone of voice and said to myself, "You are looking very beautiful tonight!" And did a little jig, ducking down elegantly, holding the hem of my skirt with both hands, bowing to myself.

I look resplendent in a peacock blue lehenga, shying away to glory. Everyone is looking at me, some with love, others with adoration and Soham like he is dazed. He is walking towards me in a nice Indo-Western attire with a diamond ring in his hand. *A ring? Shit!*

I look around frantically, trying to spot Dad, Ansh or Krish, but I see my mother happily beaming at me, smiling teary-eyed.

"Dad… Dad…" I call out as I find him, but he does not seem to hear me. *Heck!* Even I cannot hear myself.

Soham is now almost on the makeshift stage that I am standing on, ready to put that ring onto my finger. I scan the crowd for Dad once again, when I see Ronit. He is standing there, staring right back at me, his expressions conveying a series of emotions. His eyes are sad, making my heart hammer against my chest.

"Ahaana, give him your hand," Mom says, almost cooing. *No no no!*

She is taking my hand and placing it onto his. I panic, searching frantically for Ronit again, but he is gone. I jerk my hand away from Soham's and turn to run away when everything suddenly starts spinning. I am getting absorbed into a huge whirlpool, frightened to my core. A loud scream emanates from my throat when I hear my name being called out from the oblivion – *Ahaanaaa...* A loud thud follows and then again... *Ahaanaa...*

It sounds like my mother.

"Maa... Wh... What!" I jolt up, my breathing heavy.

What the hell was that! A dream?

I am insane! Everything that's happening is insane. I threw my hands up when I heard another loud thud at the door.

"Ahaana! Open the door," my mother shouted through the thick door. *Thick,* I thought exasperated.

"It is open, Mom," I shouted back.

"I have been knocking for so long!" Mom said as she charged inside.

"You could've just tried opening it," I muttered.

"Yeah! Your remark is forgiven since you let Soham drop you back home last night," she said smiling appreciatively at me which made me shut my eyes tight with irritation.

"Okay! Now tell me all about yesterday!" she came straight to the point.

I looked at her in awe, only wishing that I were still dreaming.

"Mom, I have just got up and this is not exactly what I want to talk about the first thing in the morning."

"This is morning only for you because it is already eight and most of us are already done with our breakfast and morning tea." She eyed me curiously.

"But it *is* morning for me, right? So will you please let me be?"

"I have been waiting for you to wake up since god knows when, Ahaana. The least you could do is tell your *concerned mother* about last night. I am sure you must have had a great time. Tell me how you feel about him?" she prompted.

The way she said *your concerned mother,* trying to get all that emotional blackmail in place, hitting it just at the right spot, made me exhale loudly.

"Yes! Now I am prying as well," she said with a frown.

"Okay Ma! Since you should know, it was not Soham who dropped me last night."

"What? But that did not look like Ansh? Then who was it?"

"It was Ronit!"

"Ronit? Who Ronit? You have a boyfriend and you didn't tell me? The least you could have done is save us all this humiliation. So this is the reason why you do not like Soham? What does this Ronit do? Where is he from? Do you think he will keep you happy in the future? Now I don't even know what reply I will give to the Sehgals. Oh god!"

It sounded so dramatic that I wanted to laugh it off, though I knew my mother better. Aghast at how everything was going I shrieked holding both my palms over my ears. "Stop it Maa! I am not in love with anybody. Don't you think you are being too hard on me? I want to decide certain things for myself please? I am not seeing any Ronit. He is my ex-client whose wedding we were to organise, but unfortunately his fiancé dumped him. It was a mere coincidence that yesterday's business event, which we had organised, was that of his company. And as I was heading back home, the cab that Ansh had booked for me did not arrive. *And* it was *only* because of chivalry that he drove me home," I said it all in one breath, trying to explain everything to her, which however, felt more like I was explaining things to myself.

"Oh!"

"Yes! Now if you don't mind, can I go get ready? I am running late."

"Okay! Breakfast is ready at the table." With that, she held her head high and walked out.

"Wow! Who said mothers didn't throw tantrums," I muttered.

After a quick breakfast, I headed towards office. As I neared the driveway of our workplace, I noticed a car parked right in front of the entrance. Furious at the person who did not think that the '*do not park in front of the gate*' sign applied to them as well, I collected my belongings and stormed towards it. Joshi was standing at the entrance.

"Joshi, whose car is this?" I knew I was loud, but I hated it when people disregarded basic civic sense.

"Madam ji, *ek sahib aaye hai andar aapse milne*," he replied.

I nodded at him with a smile and walked inside. I saw Ansh in a corner, staring deep into his computer screen, obviously unaware that we had a visitor. If it were a client, I figured I had to calm myself down.

Shifting my gaze to the other end, I found Mishka engrossed in some work too.

Looks like everyone is oblivious, I thought.

Looking around for the owner of the vehicle, I was stunned to see someone sitting at my desk. With his back towards me, he too seemed preoccupied. I decided to confront him myself.

"Excuse me!" I said. The man was reading a magazine, which was all right, but then who the hell was he?

Irritated now, I went over to the other side of my desk and said a little loudly this time.

"Excuse... Oh, hi Soham!" I said groaning inwardly as he turned, surprised at first and then a smile spreading across his face.

"Hey Ahaana! I have been waiting for you to arrive." He grinned.

"I am sorry, ran a little late today. Is there anything important that makes you come here so early?" As I spoke, I looked towards Ansh who was back at his desk and was giving me a rather scrutinising look, annoying me further.

"Well yeah! Actually, I was thinking if you could spend the day with me?"

Averting my gaze from Ansh, I answered absently, "Sure!"

"Really? Cool then, where would you like to go? I mean, you know the city much better. Though if you would like me to plan it up, I shall do the research quickly and make it special."

"Huh? What are you talking about?" Now he had all my attention.

"Well, you just said yes." Soham stared back, his forehead creased with confusion.

"Yes for what? I thought I told you that we wouldn't decide to marry so fast. Not until we know each other," I said as a matter of fact.

"Right and for that we *would* have to spend some time together? And that is what I approached you with to which you said yes!"

"Oh! Did you? And I said yes?"

He simply narrowed his eyes, wearing a bemused expression.

"I am sorry. Actually I am quite preoccupied, so can I plan something for later?" That wasn't going right. Clearly, I was being rude.

"But you just arrived here, Ahaana!"

"Yeah! But I have a lot of work for today!" I glanced again at Ansh for some help and this time both he and Mishka were concentrating hard on what they were doing. I stared on, trying to stress my point, but they both winced, stressing that I should go. Ansh followed it up with another glare stressing that I was being pathetically rude.

I gulped looking back at Soham. "Umm... all right, we will... eh...meet up! But can we just restrict it to lunch? Er... that is because I genuinely do have a lot of work."

"Hey, that is fine. I will pick you up at about one?"

"Yeah! Uhh… actually by one thirty, and I will have to get back early."

"That is fine, Ahaana."

I eyed him, trying to drop a hint to proceed, but he was simply looking down.

I cleared my throat thinking what to say next. "Eh… ahemm… Soham, I will see you then?"

"Oh right!" He looked up at me, with something like an expectation in his eyes. I looked away awkwardly.

"Bye!" he nodded as he turned around to leave.

Feeling foolish, I did not want to confront my friends and simply went behind my table turning on my computer. As I saw Ansh approaching, I immediately took my phone and pretended to be on a call. He seemed to buy that I was busy and walked back.

The rest of the afternoon was spent in tallying accounts and getting in touch with other clients. I did not want to talk to anybody and seriously had no intentions of thinking about anything at all. My nightmare of the morning was stark enough and I did not want to dwell into anything that reminded me of it. Whatever my future held for me, I would prepare myself to face it and I would most definitely not allow myself to do something that I was unwilling to do.

It was already one and Soham would be here any moment. As I began wrapping up my work, I sent Ansh a message saying that I had emailed the updated accounts sheet to him and also that I would be leaving. Instead of replying, he came towards my desk and sat down on the chair across me.

"Rahul had called!" he began.

"Yeah? He is here?" I asked interested.

"Yep. He wanted to talk to you, but then something came up and he had to hang up."

"Not a problem. What was he saying? When is he here?"

"Tomorrow."

"Great! So are we meeting him?"

"Yeah, for dinner tomorrow."

"That would be nice. I guess he will be announcing his engagement," I said brightly.

"He is getting engaged?" Ansh asked surprised.

"Oh no! I am just hoping that it would be that." *Oops!*

"Really?" Ansh queried, sensing something was amiss.

"Hmm… okay then, I am leaving for lunch." I waved goodbye and walked ahead, without looking back.

I waited at the entrance for Soham to arrive. It had been more than five minutes and yet, there was no sign of him. *Could he have forgotten?* Maybe there had been changes to the plan that I was unaware of, or maybe he was busy and didn't have the time to cancel our date! *Date?* I mentally whacked myself on terming this casual lunch that. Though the idea of it being cancelled did make me feel better.

"You're still here!" I hadn't heard Mishka approach.

"Yeah, the guy makes me wait. One minus point!" I made a gesture of a cross sign in the air.

She giggled saying, "Yeah! Let me know how he makes up for it and make sure you give him a plus for that!"

"Let's hope he doesn't." I winked as I said it.

"Oh c'mon Ahaana, give him a chance at least! I mean, the guy has come down all the way here so that he can win your heart. It is so obvious that he adores you." Saying that, she mocked a tick in the air, imitating me.

"Just so you know, we mutually decided against the engagement and he came here for business."

"You really think so? It is all business? It is written all over his face that he cares for you, but becomes a nervous wreck when he confronts you." Mishka smiled.

I looked away, not wanting to assimilate that bit of information.

"Why don't you call him?"

"Yeah, I think I will do that," I said as I fumbled with my phone.

As she left, I wondered what is it with friends and facts, and hitting it right across your face.

I was still thinking, standing there, when suddenly, my cell phone vibrated.

"I am terribly sorry Ahaana! I know I am being a complete jerk."

"You are not that bad." I kidded.

"Well yes! You obviously are being nice to me."

"Umm... so what now? Lunch cancelled?"

"Oh, don't say that. Actually I have been stuck with a work obligation and that is the reason for me running late. But most definitely, I will not allow anything to steal my opportunity to have lunch with you."

"Well... Okay! Now with that said, I think for that to happen, you will have to be here?"

"Of course! And I most definitely will, but it is just that... eh... if you could please proceed to the restaurant and I leave from here and meet you there directly?" As I contemplated the idea, he suddenly said, "Okay never mind, I will be there, just give me an extra five minutes please?" He was talking like he had done a big blunder. I felt bad at having that effect on him.

"Calm down! I know you only mean better as obviously that will save our time. "

"Yes, that is exactly my point," he replied with a sigh of relief.

"So I will see you there in like ten minutes?"

"Ten sounds great!"

Getting into my car, I drove towards the Taj. With the thick traffic, I barely managed to reach on time, being profusely delayed. Looking at the way the parking lot was packed towards saturation, it felt like the entire elite crowd of Bangalore had decided to come for a luncheon at the same time. I reluctantly stepped out of my car. Thinking better of it, I dialled Soham's number. He answered in the first ring.

"Hi, are you here? I am standing at the parking lot."

"Ahaana, I know I am blowing up every possibility of your liking me, but I will not be able to make it at all."

"What?" I couldn't understand what he meant by that. Anger and frustration welled up inside me and I was doing everything in my capacity to stay calm. What was he trying to do, play catch and run with me?

"The tender I was here for is suddenly going through a lot of trouble and if I as much as budge from here, I will not be able to have it. I know, no explanations count – but I am just terribly sorry," he said apologetically.

I just kept mum, not wanting to say anything that might be profane and absolutely against my character. But yeah, one thing was certainly true – he *had* blown up every chance of me liking him.

"I know you are seriously furious right now, but I have been trying to call, asking you not to leave, but your phone seemed to be unreachable. I am so sorry."

"Okay!" And with that, I simply disconnected the call. I wasn't expected to be civil when I had been waiting for almost forty-five minutes. Deciding to go back to the office, I started walking towards my car.

Ronit

Ronit saw the silhouette from behind the dark huge windows of the Taj and he knew that it was her. Somehow, he just found it way too crazy to believe that it could be a coincidence. He had been thinking about her and there she was, standing before him, feeling out of place, a delicate profile amongst all the metal. With her back towards him, she was oblivious to the fact that he was right behind and by the way she held a hand at her forehead, she seemed disturbed.

He looked around for his dad and found him engrossed in some discussion surrounded by a team of dignitaries. Everyone was busy getting business deals done and bagging contracts. He turned back to confirm if she was still standing there. She had been on a call and was now walking towards the exit. He immediately turned about and walked towards the door of the entrance and sprinted across, down the stairs towards her. She was just about to open the door of her car when he stood behind her, his hands in his pockets. Narrowing his shoulders, he bent forward and called her name softly so that he did not scare her.

"Hi Ahaana!"

She spun around unsure and with the kind of look she wore in her eyes, he figured that she had definitely expected it to be someone else. He shrugged, not quite understanding why that thought disturbed him. Clad in blue denims and a white-buttoned shirt, he admired her as her long hair flew around her face in the breeze. Tucking a silky strand behind her ears, she looked at him in utter surprise.

"Oh hi!" He was obviously not who she had expected. She seemed to be caught off-guard as he looked at the sudden appearance of tiny wrinkles on her forehead. Sensing his stare, she suddenly seemed to find her appearance important and stole a quick glance at her reflection on the window of her car. Ronit couldn't help but smile as she looked back at him.

His lips curled up with a hint of a smile as he straightened up a bit. Clearing his throat, he took one hand out of his pockets and held it out for a handshake. She took it hesitantly with a smile playing at the corners of her mouth.

"It's a pleasant surprise to see you here!" He said not taking his eyes off her for even second.

"Same here!"

"So... what brings you here? Waiting for someone?"

"Umm... no. Not really, was in fact just leaving."

"Oh! I thought I just saw you come in."

"Well yes actually, I just got here, but now will have to leave."

"Why, if I may ask?"

"I was here to meet someone who couldn't really make it."

"For lunch?"

Ahaana

Words seemed to choke within as I stared back at Ronit's familiar face. His demeanour was daunting and made me stammer. He carried himself with such confidence that he seemed to fit akin the grand architecture behind. The command in his voice almost made me feel like I owed him all the answers.

In spite of myself, I answered, "Yes, for lunch!"

"So you must not have eaten, I suppose?"

"Pretty much the thing since the friend I was waiting for did not arrive and I don't think I would want to look foolish in this place full of who is who, eating all by myself!" I pointed out as a matter of fact.

"Well, you do not have to eat alone!" He eyed me curiously, an expectant look in his eyes, making me skip a breath.

I looked at his jaws, at the darkness below his lips and how masculine he looked in that simple posture. Suddenly realizing that I was staring, I looked away. Gathering myself, I answered. "Exactly, which is why I plan to go back to my work place and have lunch with my friends."

Ronit

Ronit looked straight into her eyes, as she immediately glanced away, digging the ground below with the heel of her sandals. She was wearing almost no make-up, unlike the girls he had met so far, all ready to cover up every bit of their face with some accessory or the other, artificial colours bringing out what they did not possess. Whereas she, he thought, had him fixated on her with her natural beauty.

He did not know how to convey what he had on his mind. What if she doubted his intentions and retorted? He had never dealt with such an emotion before. He had never asked a girl out, though he knew many had a soft corner for him. But Ahaana felt so simple and yet so elegant. And right now, he meant it only as a friend *right*?

Who was he kidding though, he thought, as he realised that he was definitely attracted towards her. He could say that he had also witnessed a spark in her eyes every time they met. Going with his instincts, he propelled himself to ask her and began, "What I meant was that it wouldn't be a bad idea to consider having lunch with me? Would it?"

She raised her head as she looked up at him confused. He was dressed in formals – black blazer, trousers, a dark blue striped shirt and a silky tie, making him look like the young tycoon he was.

She had noticed his cufflinks, which had white stones studded in them that she assumed would be diamonds. Trying to decipher what he might have seen in her or could it have been that he was trying to make up in his own way for stepping back on the deal that he had made with them, she breathed in the air around him, not missing how heavy with dignity it felt. Unsure of what to say, she stammered, "You seriously don't have to go that far. We totally understand and it happens, so you don't have to feel so guilty about it!"

He looked back, staring at her with curious eyes, unsure where that came from. "What are you talking about?"

"Well... I know you feel bad about stepping back on our deal, but it is really okay. You are a wealthy man and this is probably how you go about making up for something where you did not play well, but it is not really required."

He grinned at her. "Yeah? Then how can I repay?"

"Oh, you don't have to. You went through something way more painful than a stupid deal. So really, don't worry. The other day also... you gave me a lift and now this; you shouldn't be going through all this extra trouble," she said seriously.

"Hmm... You've got a point," he said as he pretended to think it through, tapping his finger on his jaws and trying his best to suppress a grin.

"So now you can relax and carry on with your assemblage inside. It seems pretty big considering the number of visitors here."

"So you will accompany me inside, right? Now that I know you have forgiven me."

Unsure if she had heard him right, she looked back at him. "I beg your pardon?"

To that he burst out laughing, making Ahaana feel very conscious and dubious at the same time. "What?" she muttered.

"Do you really think I am trying to make up to you or something?" He laughed again as she stared back at him in confusion. Suddenly, a small smile touched the corners of her lips.

Still stifling a grin, Ronit watched her with warm eyes, as a surge of emotions took over, making him step back.

"Ahaana, when I said I think of you as a friend, I meant it. Being the jerk that I was, I did not call back since I was busy dwelling into my own animosity for whatever happened between Taashi and me. But now, I just plan to undo those mistakes. And yeah, it is nothing pretentious. I am asking you because I *want* to have lunch with you."

She searched his eyes expectantly, not missing out the easy way he had used Taashi's name, implying that he was better off without her and was no longer in the agony she had caused him. Relieved and at the same time battling with her own feelings and emotions, Ahaana simply nodded in return.

He smiled. And with that, he waited for her to step forward as he led her inside.

Ahaana

As I sauntered behind him, I could not help but notice the splendour he possessed. Confidence oozed out of every pore of his being. With the suit buttoned up, it brought out the manly lean build he possessed, showing off a narrow waist that was unimaginable for a guy to maintain with that kind of lifestyle as his.

The minute we neared the entrance, the guard was more than eager to greet him and I did not miss out on how Ronit made sure that he nodded and smiled towards him.

Realising that the colour on my cheeks was betraying me, I lost the little mettle that I had. I don't know why he had that effect on me and the thought that he *was* effecting me in this absolute foreign manner made me all the more nervous.

As we walked further into the concourse, I remembered visiting the coffee shop of the hotel once. This was one of the most prestigious properties and it definitely portrayed royalty. We neared an area that I believed was one of the restaurants of the hotel. A huge glass wall gave a view of the swimming pool on the other side. The way it blended with the interiors, it almost passed for being magical. The room was filled with a lot of guests, all sophisticatedly dressed for an occasion.

The moment we stepped inside, all the heads turned in our direction, making me very conscious. I took an involuntary step backwards, lisping a small sorry. An apologetic look immediately took over my expression and even before I could manage to back up further, Ronit quickly put a hand behind my waist and tugged me forward, leading me inside. A shot of electricity ran through me with that instant contact as I felt the warmth of his hand on my back. I looked up to find the others smiling towards him and nodding as he nodded back in return.

"They are all staring at me, right? Don't you think it's a bad idea for me to be present over here?" I whispered to him softly as I rechecked my outfit in a quick, calculative glance.

He just smiled as he pulled me closer and whispered back, "They are all delighted to see beauty in this room full of black and white men, and in no manner are you a *bad idea* for them."

I felt the colour deepen on my cheeks at his remark.

"You seem to be having a very important meeting over here. Won't they mind if you just walk out of it this way, without even excusing yourself?" I was genuinely concerned about what each one of these obviously wealthy looking people must be thinking.

"They would be glad to take a break! Now stop asking so many questions and walk a little faster please?"

I obeyed, almost sprinting along with him.

"You seem to be a very popular person!" I commented again.

"I might be," he said almost dismissing the point.

"You might be? You almost bask in the magnificence of glory!"

He looked at me then, his eyebrows raised, making me hold my breath instantly. *How can anybody have such gorgeous eyes*, I thought to myself? His eyebrows did that funny flip flap arch which I instantly remembered, making me giggle once again. He seemed to read the direction of my thoughts as he grinned back, making me go weak in my knees.

Looking away instantly, I nodded towards a table set by the pool.

We seemed to be only ones there.

"I think they are closed," I said thinking out aloud.

"Nope, please take a seat." He was about to pull my chair for me when a steward appeared from nowhere, dressed in white and black, huge hands with white gloves on. Beaming profoundly, he held a chair back for me. Smiling sheepishly, I took it and sat down as delicately as I could manage, considering all the sumptuousness.

"This place is so gorgeous! I wonder why it is empty compared to the other restaurants. I hope it is not so because of the food. Have you dined here before?" I asked him, genuinely concerned about our lunch. My apprehension made him smile again. *I wasn't being stupid, was I?*

"This place is as good as, if not better than the rest Ahaana. It is just that you are my special guest and I like privacy." The way he looked at me then made me want to melt away in my seat and I did everything I could in my calibre to stay put.

"Oh!" was all that I could manage as a reply as I tried to stay normal regardless of the way my heartbeat was going bonkers.

"So what would you like to have?" he asked.

"I think this part is just a cafeteria, so sandwiches or anything would do."

"You can have whatever you like. You prefer Chinese, right?"

"Yeah, I love Chinese!" *He remembers,* I thought and smiled incredulously.

It was as if the stewards were hiding somewhere waiting for a cue from him because all he did was just look up and two of them came over in seconds. They magically had the Chinese menu cards in their hands, which they passed over, one to both of us as they smiled and bowed down. One of them excused themselves and went away, while the other one, Shabir, as I read his nametag, stayed back to take the order.

"What can I get you to drink, sir?" he asked Ronit politely.

"Whatever my lady would prefer." He said holding out a hand in my direction, pointing towards me, making me blush.

Ronit

Hearing his own voice, Ronit shifted back on his seat. *My lady!* What was wrong with him? He knew Ahaana must have obviously found that offending. There was something about seeing her again that turned him into someone else altogether. He wanted to be as casual as he had felt the initial times that he had met her, but he just couldn't manage that around her now.

He had never known the colour crimson could dawn on anybody's cheeks that way, the way she blushed every time she looked up at him. She was dressed as casually as ever and yet she managed to look more beautiful than anybody he had ever met in his high profile life.

That's exactly what it was, he thought. She had this simplicity about her that made her look pure. The way she kept her hair, it was just so elegant. Nothing about her was pretentious and nothing that she said or did seemed made up. Everything about her was natural, delicate, and yet, she seemed so strong.

He had seen and met girls who were either exploiting their father's money, pretending that it was they who had earned it, or girls who were placed at some hierarchy or the other in various business houses, having no clue about what they were supposed to do there. They were girls who were satisfied with just looking good and not giving a second thought about content or character. This was one of the main reasons why he simply kept away from them. All they were after was his surname, his money.

But Ahaana was different. She was self-made! She was one person he had grown to respect in that small meeting a couple of months ago. She was someone who, he now had to admit, kept flashing back in his mind even when he had not kept in touch with her. And now, when she just appeared the day before, he could not get her out of his mind ever since. *Why?* He was yet to find an answer to that!

Getting a grip on himself, he cleared his throat as he spoke again. "What would you prefer? A soup or a mocktail to begin with?"

Ahaana

"Umm...," I faltered with words. "I think I will have a Mocktail... Berry Sweetheart!" I said as I pointed to the name on the menu card.

"Great choice madam! And what can I get you sir?" Shabir smiled at me before turning his attention back to Ronit.

"I will have some fresh lime please!" he said as he handed back his menu card.

"Why only a fresh lime when they have so many other interesting stuff to offer?" I asked him.

"Well, I prefer the simple one!" he said, eyeing her curiously, his lips curving at the corners.

I ignored that ingenious connotation. We placed our orders for the starters then and I unconsciously began tapping my heels on the ground as I saw Shabir leave. Ronit straightened himself on his chair as he looked at me while I fiddled with an invisible ring on my fingers, a hint of a smile brightening his features.

"So...." I began, searching for words.

Ronit looked up, like he was waiting for what I had to say.

"So... what's new?"

He simply smiled, a knowing look in his eyes. "Nothing that you would like to know, just the usual business deals and meetings." He seemed to casually choose his words, enjoying the leisure, which I assumed was a rare occasion considering the tycoon that he was.

"Oh!" I looked back down at my hand.

"And what is new with you? How are your friends?"

"They are doing great."

"That's nice! Got any weddings lined up?"

"Oh, it would have almost been mine," I muttered under my breath.

"Am sorry?"

"Uhh... no! I mean yes! There are a few events and a small wedding as well."

"Great! That must keep you preoccupied well enough."

"Absolutely!" After a pause, I continued, "How are your parents?"

"They are good. Busy in their metier."

I smiled to that as Shabir came forward with our drinks. He placed the fancy drinks on our table. I silently thanked the welcome break. I had never been at such a loss of words as I was today. Shabir left with a smile.

"So, what are your plans of settling down?" Ronit asked, taking me off guard with his direct question.

"Huh?"

"Yeah?! Don't your parents keep asking you to marry? I get placed on that spot all the time."

"Actually yes! It is the same here... all the time!" I said.

He smirked, making me want to tell him about Soham and how I was positive now that he was not the right one for me. I did not know why I wanted to share all that with him, considering the fact that we hardly shared anything more than a business relationship. Except of course, the time when Ronit allowed me into the memories of his late brother.

"What happened? What are you thinking?" he asked looking concerned over the sudden change in my expressions.

"Nothing, just remembered something."

"Yeah? What, if I may ask?"

"Uhh.... just the last time I met you."

"Goa?"

"Yes!"

"Aah, that was crazy! That was so much of confusion."

"If you can call it that," I said, a little unsure.

"You don't have to hesitate when we talk about that, Ahaana," he said looking at me square in the eye. "I am well over it."

"You should be! She was the closest thing to a catastrophe."

Ronit burst out laughing at my comment. "Well, I did not know you thought so highly of her."

"Er... I am sorry. I shouldn't have said that."

"Relax, I couldn't have cared less. I am pretty sure I have someone way better, waiting out there for me."

"So... are you waiting for her?"

He raised his eyebrows, unsure of what I was coming to. "Uhh... yes, you can say that. After all, I am turning twenty-nine and settling down isn't such a bad idea. But of course, with the right person."

"Yes, of course. With the right person!" Once again, I was racked speechless as I mentally went back to my 'almost engagement day'. I reflected on how destiny had flashed a chain of events on my face. And now, when at this time I was supposed to have been meeting Soham over lunch and considering my future with him, here I was, sitting with the person I had never thought I would meet again.

"Are you comfortable, Ahaana?" He scrutinized me, noticing the discomfort that had crept back into my expressions.

"Oh yes. I am all right. I am sorry, it is nothing. Were you saying something?" I shrugged gaping back at him.

At that same instance, Shabir came with an arrangement of our starters on a trolley, followed by another steward who delicately placed them before us as they served us the appetizers. I breathed in the aroma of the Chinese cuisine and smiled at the effect. Ronit gazed at me, looking astounded as he noticed the smile bring back the colour to my cheeks.

She definitely loves Chinese, I could almost see him make a mental declaration.

"Don't look at me that way! I revere Chinese food."

"That I can see for myself and I am glad it does that to you," he said pointing a finger at the glow on my cheeks.

"Have you ever considered donating blood?" he suddenly asked with a serious expression.

"Huh? Yes, I do that sometimes," I said, not sure where he was heading.

"Coz' you seriously do have an abundance of it. The way it rushes into your cheeks every time..." He grinned, pointing a finger towards them, making the ruddiness burn deeper.

I kept quiet looking down and then away, just trying to focus on anything but that breathtaking smile on his face.

"Now, are you flirting with me?" I tried to turn the side.

"You don't want me to?"

"Uh... not if you don't mean the flattery!" I said grinning back at him.

"Well in that case, I am entitled to flirt some more!" He said arching his eyebrows purposefully, making me laugh.

"Why does that happen to you? How can you have a control over the muscle there?" I asked looking amazed as I pointed towards his eyebrows.

"Well, on the contrary, it is something that is quite involuntary. It has just been this way ever since I remember. Initially, it used to happen every time I was nervous. For some reason, Roshan seemed to enjoy it and *that* made me let go of making any deliberate attempts to cease it from happening. I used to love it when he laughed!"

I suddenly felt horrible upon bringing it up and yet couldn't help smile as I saw him remember his brother so fondly. "I am sorry."

"Oh don't be! I like to remember Roshan every day. And I like to smile when I think of him, else he might get mad up there," he said, pointing a finger towards the sky.

I felt something snap inside at the mere expression of such pure love. To be brave this way, to remember the person you love, required a lot of courage!

"Ahaana! Thank you. I am glad you decided to come by this place." He turned his gaze away then and as if to add on some deeper meaning to his words, he stared back and said, "And more than that, I am delighted that you agreed to have lunch with me." This time he looked directly at me, making me feel every word he said.

I stared back at him and replied softly, "I think this is what I needed as well."

He nodded and looked down towards my plate. "You haven't eaten anything; our main course will be here any minute."

"Yeah!" I looked away quickly as I dug a fork into the starters on my plate.

Ronit

As they chatted about their likes and dislikes, Ronit realised that he was developing a liking towards her, more and more with each passing minute. He stared at her as she spoke affectionately about her family with an enamoured expression. She laughed as she said something and the tinkle of her laughter made him wander into some place alien altogether. He could not understand why she captivated him the way she did and did not know how to handle what he felt right then.

"I have always wanted to get married in the snow. And I think the two places that are a priority on my wish list are New Zealand and Switzerland. What do you wish for?" she was saying.

"Ronit?" She looked at him puzzled, as he did not reply instantly.

"Uh? Sorry!" He straightened up as he snapped back. "You were saying something?"

She angled her stare as she grinned and said, "I asked if you have any special wishes? Like I want to get married in a place where there is snow all around, maybe a place like New Zealand or Switzerland. Likewise, do you have any special dreams?"

"Oh? I really have not thought about that," he said plainly.

"I don't buy that. Everybody has dreams and I am sure you are not an exception. So tell me."

The way she commanded him, he smiled, feeling the hair on his skin stand in response to her presence. "Okay! As a kid I had many. I wanted to be a singer. Me and Roshan would spend hours in our outhouse, he on his guitar and me lending him the vocals."

"You sing? Wow! That is *tough* to imagine," she said grinning.

"Why? Do I look like a person with no vocal chords?" he pretended to look offended.

She giggled. "No, you just seem more of those serious kinds who just knows how to manage business and people, the workaholic species."

He laughed loudly at the way she described him, "I shall prove how wrong you can be!"

"I would love to be proven wrong, Mr Malhotra!"

He smiled back at her as he took in her presence and the warmth that she reflected.

"So why don't you start?"

"What?" he asked confused.

"Singing!"

"Huh! Have you lost it? I am not doing that *here*."

"Why? These guys are already charmed by you and I am sure they would not feel offended if you claim to be a musical treat?"

"I did not say that. I just said I *wished* to be a singer. That I am good at it was just an off-hand comment to conquer the argument we might have had."

"Well, it seems to have worked. Now if you would please honour me?"

"Ahaana!"

"Ronit!" She said mimicking his tone, looking at him right in the eye, smiling softly and that seemed to be enough for him to simply obey.

"But I haven't sung in ages."

"No problem, you'll find your voice right there!"

He made a face, making her grin. "Fine. Here goes!"

Smile an everlasting smile, a smile can bring you near to me... Don't ever let me find you gone, 'cause that would bring a tear to me...

And he went on, making Ahaana listen in awe to the soft, yet manly rhythm of his voice, goosebumps lining her skin! She listened to him go on, looking at her and then away, smiling as he sang those words from one of her all time favourites.

Na na na na na na na... na na na na na na na.

She joined him along as he sung those lines, both tapping along, unaware of the staff smiling at them with bewildered looks from behind. As he finished, Ahaana stood up for a standing ovation as she clapped and was suddenly joined by Shabir and the other stewards while they clapped on along with her. Ronit was surprised at what greeted him and smiled awkwardly as he nodded at them and said a thank you. He raised his gaze to meet Ahaana's. "Thank you," he said softly, stopping himself from raising his hands to tuck a loose strand of hair tickling her cheeks.

She chirped excitedly as she sat down. "You are not just good, you are awesome, Ronit! And you had that hidden? My god! Nobody would be able to decipher that this Mr Business tycoon is an even better singer! Why have you suppressed it all this while? You would have been an even popular playback singer by now. I mean..."

"Ahaana! Shhhh!" He said placing a finger on his lips trying to shun her to silence. "I get your point," he said as he grinned back at her.

"What do you mean? You said so, right? That this was your dream? Then what was holding you back? I mean, I don't get it!" She sat back straight on her chair, waiting for him to answer.

His expression sobered down as he took a sip of water. "They are very few."

"Huh? What?"

"I am talking about the wishes that come true."

They were interrupted when Shabir came back with the main course. Ahaana tapped her hands on the table impatiently as he served them their meal. She pounced back to what they were talking about the minute he left them alone again.

"Yeah, so you were saying something about wishes not coming true!"

"Do you have to be so particular? I mean, you have your *Chinese* in front of you, why bother about something that insignificant?" He grinned again.

"I don't know, but I would like to know what held you back when you clearly have such an amazing voice."

"Oh! Why did I even heed to your request!" He mocked exasperation.

"That's rude!" She said narrowing her eyes at him.

"Okay! Eat, and I will indulge you with my stories in between."

"That is better," she said, twirling strands of noodles on her fork as she waited for him to begin.

"I loved singing and took quite a few classes as well. In fact, Dad supported too. Roshan also loved his guitar and would join me. I have also done a few stage shows back in college."

To that Ahaana raised an eyebrow, surprised but let him continue.

"But then, after he left, I left music as well. He was the rhythm Ahaana and I did not like singing without having him listen to me or play along with me. I left it for him and business was something like an obvious platform I would eventually adapt to. And thus, I took it. Simple!"

Again, she was shunned to silence as she looked down, feeling foolish and stupid at the same time. This was the second time today that she had made him remember his brother and hurt him.

"I... I am so terribly sorry! I shouldn't have even brought it up. I am such a douche."

He grinned. "Okay. If you insist."

She raised her head, tangled in her own thoughts as she managed a smile. "Sorry," she muttered again.

"I am kidding... it's fine."

"That means you will sing more often now?"

He stared at her unbelievingly, at the sheer possibility of such a unique make by the creator! "You do not give up, do you?"

"Nope! Perhaps that is why I do what I do."

He nodded his head in agreement as they both burst into splits of laughter. Their eyes were moist by the time they stopped laughing. Ronit coughed up, placing a closed fist to his mouth as he raised his eyes towards her. She smiled back at him as she played with her fork.

"Will I be seeing you again?" He looked, searching for a change of expression, but her smile remained intact.

"Yes," she said as she stared into her plate and then glimpsed back up at him.

"Good," he said as he sat back and relaxed on his chair.

Ahaana

"Hah!" I exclaimed with a sigh as I stopped my car at a corner on the main road. I had had one of the most extraordinary times of my life and I still could not fathom how it had found me.

Ronit had escorted me towards my car with the same dignity as he had taken me inside that restaurant an hour ago. Once again, I had felt all eyes staring at me curiously as we were on our way out, but this time, they did not unnerve me. I had wanted to exit from the other side, not wanting to face the delegates who knew Ronit well enough. He was almost like a superstar back there, yet, on second thoughts, I chided myself, he seemed like no one less. I recalled our conversation again and again.

"What is wrong now?" he had asked, standing like a man very near the limit of his patience.

"If you must know, the idea of walking back in there with the people thinking what they are thinking," I had given an expressive shudder.

"Do not fret Ahaana! All that they must be doing is envying my luck." He had winked, making his point clear as I shook my head in disapproval.

"C'mon Ronit, please let's just take the other way out. What harm would it do to you? I don't want to be scrutinised all over again."

"Ahaana!" he had pulled me by the arm, leaving my skin tantalized by his touch, the shiver running all the way up. Stopping short of re-entering the convention room, I had halted. "We can't go in together."

"Let me guess." Ronit rolled his eyes. "What will people think?"

I blushed recalling how he had ignored and pulled me all the way out, holding me by my waist. As I had got inside my car, he stood next to me, leaning at the door and had looked down at me with a smile, saying, "I will call you". All that I could manage then was a measly little nod as I put on the ignition and drove away, watching his reflection get smaller and smaller.

I had been driving for about ten minutes, with as much as a little breathing to keep me alive. When I finally couldn't take the blood rushing through my veins so frantically, I had decided to halt my car at a corner.

What would all of this add up to? I thought to myself as the reality of my life hit me with force. I realised that it was Soham with whom I was bound with an obligation and a promise. And here I was, getting weak knees for a man whose wedding I was going to arrange in the recent past, someone who was supposed to be nobody but an ex-client. And that was to be the only connection that I should be sharing with him.

I remembered the first time when Ronit had walked into my office and recalled staring at him like he had just walked out from a dream. I remembered our lunch at The Serenity, the little disclosure of his heart about his brother, the freedom I had felt when I had laughed my head off with him at his expressions. I remembered the pain that had instilled upon me when he said that his wedding had been called off. And I remembered his name being announced at the Mumbai airport. I remembered all of it – all of it in a lot of detail!

I thought back on our lunch. Was all that a pretention, a welcome break from that business meet of his? Or was I actually someone who could be a little more? The latter was what I intuited when I saw the look in his eyes when he had questioned if we would be seeing each other again. But again, I wasn't sure and somewhere deep within, guilt was gorging up on my insides. I could not decide what to do or what to feel.

At one end was Soham, who had actually been trying to get me to like him, but for some reason, was failing to even be able to meet me. And here, on the other end, was Ronit, who was unaware of what I had begun to feel for him.

Maybe I was being absurd, crazily stupid! I felt like I was flying every time that I was with him and *that* was just not fair! Maybe, just maybe I must give Soham a chance to express himself, while I myself must try to give him some of my time. And then maybe, I should wait for destiny to play its turn. But as I thought all of that, I still couldn't help but think about Ronit and the way my heart throbbed when I was around him.

I decided to let destiny do what it felt was right for me while I would do what I felt was right. With that, I dialled Soham's number. I did not have a chance to think of anything else as he answered the call immediately.

"Hi Ahaana! I am so sorry," I heard him.

"I am sorry as well Soham. I was way too rude to you when you genuinely had a problem."

"I should have just told you about being held up for the tender, but I really did not want to have another day wasted by not meeting you. So I insanely tried to stuff our lunch in, hurting you in the process."

"It is all right Soham. I understand," I said, trying to shun the negative feeling in my head.

"Thanks a ton Ahaana. You don't know how relieved you make me feel by saying that. I will most definitely make it up to you."

"That will not be necessary!" I said, rather too quickly.

"Why not! I was such a maniac."

"Soham. I want to tell you something."

Shit! Here it goes! I gritted my teeth nervously as my mind and heart suddenly decided upon the same thing. I tried to ignore the crazy palpitations in my chest because of what I was about to do. Trying to muster up the strength to say what I suddenly intended to, I tried to find the right words.

"What is it, Ahaana?"

Something about the tone of his voice told me that he seemed to have guessed what I had in mind.

"Soham, I really like you... uh..." I hesitated.

"You do?" he asked seeming suddenly hopeful, leaving me hopelessly confused.

"I mean, I... I really like you, but only as a friend." I paused, suddenly aware of what I was about to say. Wondering if he had understood what I meant, I tried to continue but words refused to come. I still didn't know where my thoughts were coming from and on what basis was I deciding to do this. But I did know one thing for sure, that I did not feel for Soham the way he wanted me to and would not, in the future either.

"I am really sorry Soham, but I have tried. I do not want to make an attempt of liking someone, especially not the person who I am going to marry."

He still did not say anything, which made me want to suddenly say another sorry and hang up.

"I get it. I am sorry for wasting your time."

"Hey please! I know I am not particularly your favourite person at the moment, but if we had to be together, we would have clicked from the start."

"That is why I feel sorry."

"Please, I already feel terrible Soham. Really."

"Ahaana, I do understand. Carry on and wish you all the luck in life."

I did not know how to respond to that as I dug my fingernails into my closed fist.

"I just am sorry."

"Me too. Take care," he said and hung up.

I stared nervously at my phone, like it had just witnessed my most monstrous behaviour. Feeling nauseated, I took a deviation, leaving the route towards my office behind and heading on the path that led me home.

"What the hell is wrong with you?" Ansh said blatantly on the other end of the phone.

"Nothing. I am sorry. Just not feeling well, so decided to get back home."

"Look, I think we really have to talk now. All right?"

I simply kept quiet, not willing to go there at all. "Did something happen at lunch with Soham?" he asked.

I had decided and I did not want to discuss it with anyone. Not even with Ansh right then.

"No Ansh, nothing happened and I am sorry, but please can I talk to you later? I am really not in the mood."

"Okay! If that's what you want."

Immediately, I felt like the monster again, the one who was breaking the second heart in a day and I tried to retrieve my words. "Ansh, I am sorry. I have just not been myself lately."

"Hmm. That we all can see. So would you now tell me what happened at your lunch with Soham?"

"Nothing! He did not turn up at the hotel either. He had some tender that he had to suddenly look after."

"He stood you up?"

"I wouldn't put it that way. It was all right... he had work and he could not come."

"Hmm... so you did not have lunch at all?"

I conflicted within myself whether I should tell him or not and then not finding any harm in it, I said, "I had lunch."

"You did? So you went home directly from there? Are you really all right sweetheart?"

I could feel the worry in his voice and felt a smile creep up, glad that he was there as always.

"Ansh, I am fine and I had lunch at the Taj... with Ronit!"

"Ronit? Ronit Malhotra?"

"Yes!"

"Oh! How did that work out?" he asked after a small pause.

"He was there attending a convention at the same time and he happened to see me. It was lunch hour, so he invited me in."

"I see... and how did it go?"

"It went well!"

"Did you happen to speak with Soham again later?" His tone was weird and that made me wonder what was going on in his mind.

"Yes."

"Good."

I smiled remembering how Ronit had used the same words earlier and unintentionally blushed at the memory. It was as if my mood swing was visible through that phone when Ansh asked, "What happened?"

"Nothing! Umm…. I need to tell you something."

"Yes? I am listening?"

I knew that Ansh was being very careful with me right now and I also knew that he was worried. I did not even blame him for that. I was aware that he cared for me.

"I told Soham that I will not marry him. Like a full and final thing."

He was silent, just as I had expected him to be.

I opened my mouth to say something more when he impeded, "So you feel happy now? Relaxed?"

Now that was a good question! I thought, feeling furthermore awful about myself. Maintaining my silence, I let Ansh continue.

"Listen, you do not need to pretend with me, all right? If you have forgotten, then let me remind you that I have known you for twenty years now. Yeah? This *may be* the worst sort of predicament that you've had to face in life, but it happens with everyone. So do you mind cutting yourself some slack and telling me a little more about Ronit, the way you know him, now?"

I heard the hint of a smile and felt like recoiling within myself. How could he know me like that… *Why* did he know me like that, I complained to myself.

"Ronit? Umm… I haven't really thought about that. I just have to first think about telling my parents about what I have told Soham. For all you know, Mom is going to boycott me altogether."

I fell silent but then thinking of something else, I continued, "You know what Ansh? I really do not care now. I have decided and that will be it. I tried and am not able to get myself to think of a future with him. My parents would understand that. Hell, they should!"

"Yep!"

"What yep? Tell me how will I tell them?" I shrieked.

"Just tell them everything frankly, like how you told me. And by the way, the way things are happening, they will not be upset for a long time," he said, hinting at the obvious hidden facts from me.

"What do you mean?" I pretended not to understand.

"Never mind. It shall dawn upon you soon."

"I don't know what you are talking about."

"Ahaana, I know a lot more than you have given me credit for."

"I don't care," I snapped. "I will call you later."

"Sure! By the way, Rahul is in town, remember? I have confirmed for lunch tomorrow. You are in, right?"

"Yes, I am."

"Okay! Rest then, and let me know when you need a shoulder."

"Why would I?" I raised an eyebrow, getting restless with the way he seemed to not just pretend, but also, actually *know* everything.

"You are going to tell your parents about dumping Soham, right?"

"I did not dump him. I just said no to his proposal."

"Put it that way if you must, but make sure you don't keep them on the edge for long. Bye."

"I will tell them," I replied softly as he hung up.

I knew he was right. I had to tell my parents everything. I had to tell them now!

It was beyond midnight and I couldn't get myself to sleep, simply because the events of the day had churned my insides beyond repair. Firstly, Soham not showing up for lunch. That followed by the sudden aggression convulsing into a complete surprise upon meeting Ronit, something that I was still coming to terms with. The call of denial to Soham and then the hour when I faced my parents, especially mother, about not wanting to marry Soham and not even considering the proposal. *Actually, no!* When I told her that I had already spoken to Soham and dismissed him completely... *that* topped the list.

I had already known what the repercussion of my confession would be as I listened to each of Mom's wrath-filled words, one after the other. It was only later when I got into the warm embrace of my room did I feel a little better.

Ronit

Lying lazily on his back, Ronit was staring at the wooden panelled ceiling. Any other night, he would have been working on some deal or the other, thinking about how to maximise his returns. That night, however, was different, as he did nothing but blankly replay the afternoon, again and again in his mind.

He did not know what this feeling was and his pragmatic attributes failed him. He knew he was getting attracted towards Ahaana and he also knew the repercussions of that. His analytic mind began calculating the odds of her liking him back. She was a girl who was self-made and Ronit was certain that she would want a man who she could take pride in. He was afraid that his wealthy background might cause her to dismiss him as a man with an ego as big as his bank account.

Judging based on his conviction, his heart brought him back to their coincidental meeting that day. He remembered the glint in her eyes as she sang with him, sure that she was cheerful and friendly and playing along with her carefree attitude. But then it was nothing that was not similar to the last time he had seen her. Maybe she was simply being generous to him, considering the past. But yes, he was thinking and rather hoping for something more.

He smiled at the memory of their first meeting. He pictured her from there and remembered her from today; and in both places, he remembered seeing her high cheekbones showing off the crimson colour. The fact that he had made her blush, made his heart swell with unexpected pleasure.

He was still thinking about her when he felt his cell phone vibrate beneath him. For a split second, he hoped that it would be her, that with some divine interference, she would call him. But his spirits died down just a little as he saw who the caller was. He voiced a soft greeting.

"Hi Soham!"

"Hey buddy!" He seemed to mimic his own mood and that made Ronit a little alert.

"What's up? Is something wrong?"

He kept quiet as Ronit waited for him to speak up. He knew Soham was in town and had met him just once on the day of the orientation programme where he had invited him. Thinking about the day rushed back the memories of his encounter with Ahaana. He sighed at the thought and tried to concentrate upon what Soham was telling him.

"She simply said a no dude!" Lost in his own thoughts, Ronit caught the last words.

"Who? I am sorry, I did not get that. Did you give out the mystery girl's name to me finally?" He kidded, a smile forming at the corners of his mouth.

"I didn't, though it does not hold any mystery anymore."

"What are you talking about Soham? What happened?

"Nothing buddy, I think I will call you later. Okay?" With that, he abruptly hung up! Ronit stared at the screen unbelievingly. Soham never behaved that way. Okay, he did not pay attention to what he was saying, but then he couldn't just get mad at him for that. He redialled his number, but it was switched off.

At first he thought of going to see him, but then it struck him that he did not know where Soham was staying. He had shifted out from the hotel that he had checked in on the day he had arrived due to distance issues from his client office. Thinking about meeting him the next day, he took a deep breath and decided to sleep.

Only this time, he imagined Ahaana asleep, with a peaceful smile spread across her face and that was all that he needed to close his eyes in peace. He knew his friend was troubled about something, but then, there was another realisation that was dawning upon him – that he was most definitely, unexpectedly falling in love!

Ronit got up early, though he had hardly caught any sleep. He smiled and got out of his bed to get ready for the day. He knew he had to meet Ahaana and disclose what he felt for her. He would obviously give her time to think and knew it was sudden, so he was also prepared for a minimal wait, if not an outright rejection, which he hoped would not really happen. After taking a quick shower, he left for his office to meet the few clients who could not be avoided.

It was afternoon by the time he finished and before he went to meet her, he thought he'd call her up. He scrolled through his contact list and found her number. Just as he was about to hit the dial key, Soham called. Suddenly feeling guilty upon missing out on his priorities, he took the call.

"Hey dude! I am really sorry I could not get back. What was wrong with you last night?" he tried sounding as casual as possible, unable to stop the flutter in his stomach for an entirely different reason.

"A lot is Ronit, but talk to me only if you have a while to spare," he sounded upset and Ronit did not have to guess what the reason was.

"I am sorry man! I was just pre-occupied when you had called and even before I could explain, you hung up!"

"Okay, I agree I was not particularly easy myself. Now where are you?"

"Uhh... I was just leaving from work." He hesitated before going on.

"Okay, I will see you in five minutes outside your building." He was almost commanding and Ronit did not think it was the best idea to refuse just then.

Ronit looked at his watch that showed well half past two, making him realise that time was running out. He had thought of meeting Ahaana for lunch, ensuring he would not be prying during work hours.

Never mind! He thought. *The day is still long.*

As he waited impatiently in his lobby, he spotted Soham get off from his rented car and walk towards him. His eyes were cold and his face almost expressionless. He still managed a weak smile as Ronit greeted him.

"What's gotten into you? Just look at you! You look like someone has beaten you up in the gut!" Concern was an understatement to what Ronit felt as he looked at his friend.

"Yup buddy. I do need a friend and am sorry for bossing around. But no one else can help."

"Relax buddy, I am all ears."

"The girl, who I was here to see, she rejected me!"

Ouch! Ronit thought as he remembered the feeling Soham was talking about.

"She did?" He was genuinely angry now. "What the hell is wrong with these girls? What has got into them that they think they can just whack any man's heart the way they want to?"

Soham twitched his lips an instant, almost smiling at the melodramatic manner in which Ronit had put it.

"Okay fine! I know you have been there, done that, sort of a thing, but don't exaggerate now."

"I am not dude! I don't have words for such people."

"Relax, but *that* is not my problem."

"Huh? I don't understand." Ronit sounded perplexed, not knowing where all of this was heading.

"The problem is that I have…. uhh…" he looked away, making Ronit roll his eyes.

"Don't tell me you have fallen in love with this girl."

He simply gazed back at him, not saying anything but just nodding a yes.

"Wow!" Ronit threw up his hands in exasperation. "Dude! She is definitely not worth it. I mean, she said no to you twice. Get the hint buddy. Move on!"

"I don't know how to do that. All I can think of is *her*, be it work or no work."

"What blew it up? Hadn't you guys decided to spend some time together? You know… getting to know each other better?"

"It wasn't her. I blew up things!" He looked down again.

"What?! Oh okay! Fine, calm down." He paused and then sat down on the sofa, gesturing Soham to sit down as well. "Now what exactly did you do?" Ronit tried.

"Well, I had asked her out for lunch and stood her up!"

"That is all? And she rejected you?"

"No dude! It *was* my fault. I did mess it up. I gave her a time and said that I would pick her up and I did not turn up, yet she waited. Then I gave her another time and place and made her wait and yet could not turn up, and this time she blew up!"

"Hmm!" Ronit thought as he rubbed his chin, thinking about what he had just heard. It was almost like he was on a prowl for a judgment.

"Do you think she liked you? Did you feel it?"

Soham looked away then and simply said, "No."

"But you are in love with her?"

"Most definitely. All I want is to at least let her know that, but I have lost that chance as well." Soham looked like he had been slapped.

"Relax Soham! Don't be so hard on yourself. I have a feeling that this girl will come back to you."

"You think so?" He looked up at him hopefully.

"Yeah dude, positive!" He grinned as he playfully pressed a slap on his back. "Just give her some time."

"Thanks man. I guess that makes me feel better." He smiled back.

"Good! Now what is her name?" Ronit grinned as he asked that question.

"Agarwal!" Soham said teasingly.

"Great, I am listening, go on," he said as he leaned in a bit, bringing his ears closer, "the full name please?"

Ahaana

I was sitting absently between Ansh and Rahul as I stared at my phone, half expecting Ronit to call. We were out for lunch instead of dinner as Rahul had some change in his plan at the last moment. Rahul and Ansh were busy catching up with the usual boyish charm while I was sitting and contemplating on calling Ronit. I simply could not concentrate on anything or anyone, but the thoughts that kept taking me back to him.

"Ahaana! If you could stop day dreaming now, then I have something that I want to tell you guys."

"Huh?" I snapped back as I locked the keypad of my smartphone. "I am sorry, I was just thinking about something."

"Yeah! We could see that," Ansh put in as I gave him a cautious glare.

"Okay! Forget that. What were you saying?" I looked at Rahul.

"I am getting married!" He threw up his arms as a wide grin spread across his features.

"Wow!" Ansh and I shrieked in unison.

Ansh literally jumped off his chair as he embraced Rahul in a friendly hug while I waited my turn, smiling happily for my friend. When they parted, I walked towards Rahul, giving him a big hug. I went back to the time when we, as teenagers, sat and discussed what it would it be like when we would be married. And today, here we were, beginning to live that moment.

"Dude, you were hiding this news from me all this while?" Ansh gave a playful punch on his stomach while Rahul tried to save himself from it, making me I giggled at their boisterous playfulness.

"Ahaana, you already knew about her right? And you... *et tu Brute!!*" Ansh said looking towards us, mocking anger.

"Brilliant news Rahul! Just ignore this idiot. And now we have to speak with Meera," I said, elated.

"Sure Ahaana, I will make you guys talk to her."

Ansh was still pretending to be offended as Rahul and I burst into splits of laughter.

"C'mon buddy! Now is not the time to fulfil your dreams of becoming a pain in the wrong place, so just cope with us." This time Rahul was the one to place a playful punch on his stomach.

Rahul dialled Meera's number on his cell phone and we both spoke to her one after the other.

I could not stop grinning as I saw the look of fulfilment on my friend's face. It was almost contagious.

"She is great Rahul!" I said fondly as we hung up. "An absolute darling."

"Thanks Ahaana!"

"Yeah dude, she sounds great. I actually think you deserve someone like her." Ansh patted him on his back fondly, making Rahul's smile grow wider.

"Have you guys decided upon the dates?"

"Yes. November it is!"

"Brilliant!"

I sighed as I took a sip of my mocktail, recalling the two crazy things that this November had scheduled for me, but now was void of either of the events. One, a cancelled wedding that we were to plan, something that somehow got me *too* warmed up to someone; two, an almost wedding of myself with someone I could not fathom sharing my life with and from which I withdrew, rather uncharacteristically.

I looked up at the clock from my desk as I packed my belongings, retiring for the evening. After our lunch with Rahul, Ansh had taken an off for the rest of the day and had gone out with him while I had decided to get back to work. It was almost 7.30 and Mishka had already left. I waited for Joshi to leave with the rest of the staff, as I had to lock the main gates before I headed home.

It had been yet another tiring day and all I wanted to do was simply catch onto some sleep.

"Madam ji, you can close the office," Joshi said.

"Okay." I nodded as he left. I gathered whatever was left behind on the table and taking one last glance at my computer, I shut it down. Just as I was about to leave I realised that the shutter needed some help while closing and I would never be able to do it all alone.

"Uggh! How could I forget?" I cursed, gritting my teeth, angry at my absentmindedness. I called for Joshi to stop, but even before I could make it to the door, he was off on his bike.

"Darn it!" I swore out aloud.

Walking back inside, I took my bag and turned off the lights. I closed the main entrance glass door and locked it. Placing my bags on the side, I stood on my toes as I held the latch of the aluminium shutter and tried to pull it down with all the strength I possessed. It did not even budge.

I tried again, but in vain. Fuming, I rubbed my palm together to ease out the burning.

"Need some help?"

"Huh?" I jumped at the sudden sound. I spun around, startled at the intrusion, although already matching the voice with that of its owner. My mouth was ajar in surprise and the moment I realised that, I shut it immediately.

"Uh..." My heart fluttered uncontrollably. I tried to control my already erratic breathing as Ronit stared directly into my eyes with an intensity that held onto my gaze, making it impossible to look away.

Ronit stepped forward, only an inch away from me as he held the latch, brushing my fingers with his, making me withdraw my hand immediately in response to the electrifying touch. I jerked back, while he, with as much as a little effort, pulled down the shutter.

Still faltering for words or reason, I stood there uprooted as he turned around to face me, a broad smile brightening his already handsome features. I groaned inwardly, shouting at myself for gaining some composure as my knees wobbled in spite of my warnings.

"Hhh... Hi..." I stammered, irritated at being so out of control in front of him.

"Hi! I guess I caught you at the right hour," he said eyeing the shutter.

"Oh, yes. That you did!" I said shifting uncomfortably. The effect his presence had on me was written on my face, making me shudder with apprehension as I looked away. His gaze did not falter for a moment as I felt him read my expressions.

He crossed his arms over his broad chest, the muscles at the forearm stretching, showing off the strength they possessed. Clad in denims and a black t-shirt, he did not help in my futile attempts of holding my composure. *Damn! He was handsome.*

Ronit cleared his throat as I shifted my gaze to meet his eyes, that were staring back at me with an intensity I tried to fight.

"What brings you here?" I recoiled at the way my voice croaked.

"You did!" he replied, not bothering to look anywhere else but directly into my eyes.

I felt sweat dab on my palm as I wiped my hands on my trousers, all the while wondering how to react.

Was he here to say what I had been hoping for all through the day and all of last night? In fact, if I did not lie to myself, what I had wanted since the first time I set my eyes on him?

"Would you give me company for dinner tonight?" he asked casually, although I saw him scraping a smidgen of mud from the heels of his shoes on a tiny piece of stone. *That wasn't nervousness, was it?*

"Uhh… I have my car… emm… and I… I don't…" struggling to find the right words that would make sense, I nervously tried to make an excuse, even though all I wanted to say was a yes!

"My driver will take it for you."

"Oh! Would he?"

"Yes? So now can you come along?" There was a hint of a smile on his perfect face which made me want to melt away right there.

"Okay! I will. But umm… I think I would like to change first… that's because of the kind of places you dine at." I added meekly, suggesting our last encounter.

"I think you look beautiful, Ahaana… At least, *I* cannot take my eyes off you." *He sure as hell knows how to flirt.*

"I think that is an overstatement." I was dressed in a pair of black formal trousers and a satin maroon full shirt. Though it was a completely formal garb, I was a little conscious that it was similar to what I was wearing when we had last met during the convention, making me doubt my outfit again. But I knew better than to fuss over something that unimportant as I took his lead and sat down on the front seat while he politely held the door for me.

"May I have your car keys please?" he asked holding his hand forward. I instantly dug my hands into my purse, nervously finding my keys, and placed them onto his outstretched palm with not as much as a glance towards him. He took them swiftly as he handed them over to his driver, giving him fast instructions. Closing my door, he then walked in a captivating grace, over to the other side. He sat next to me, making me suddenly aware of the closed space around us as he stared at me, his expressions unreadable.

I heard him inhale sharply as he looked ahead with another smile while he took charge behind the wheels.

"Shall we?" He smiled as he looked at me once again and keyed in the ignition.

"Where are we going?"

"Just some place I wanted to go since a long time but couldn't get the right opportunity."

"And what is it called?" I glanced up towards him but his gaze was fixated on the road ahead.

"It is a cafeteria and I thought you might like it as well."

"Okay!"

I kept mum the entire journey, just exchanging a few words with him and not really saying anything but simply concentrating on the road.

I was familiar with the area. It was a broad highway surrounded by lush greenery on either side, popular as the ring road. As the car screeched to a halt, I recognised the place instantly. It was one of my favourite coffee shops that stood not too far from the main city and yet on the outskirts.

With a peaceful quietness and an outdoor setting, the place attracted many customers. There was a cover of lush green grass and over it was a pathway of rough stones, leading to various seating arrangements made at intervals. There were tiny blue and yellow light strings all around the setting, making it look like tiny stars falling onto the ground. The cafe also had an indoor setting with huge glass walls.

I had been there a couple of times and had always marvelled at the peacefulness it brought within me. It was a place I would come to when I craved some solitude and it would work wonders. A place like this was ideal for making the simple moments in life, really special.

Feeling ecstatic, I walked in beside Ronit. We took a table in the open area, adorned with spectacular landscaping and lighting.

Overhead was a huge umbrella which gave it a very rustic appeal. There were only a few more people around, couples to be more precise, considering the cosy manner in which they sat and looked adoringly at one another. I blushed again as I looked at the man beside me. He stared back knowingly, making me look away, as I began fidgeting with the string of my handbag nervously.

A steward stepped before us, approaching to pull a chair for me when Ronit stopped him and stepped forward.

"Allow me!" He held out the chair, looking at me. I could feel the blood rush onto my cheeks as I took it. Ensuring I was comfortable, he settled down across from me. Handing over our menu cards, the steward nodded and left us.

There was a dimly lit candle before us, making room for a serene effect on our faces. I swallowed as I inhaled sharply, trying to calm myself down, not willing to go on a roller coaster ride of feelings at that very moment.

Ronit

As the candlelight brought out a soft glow on her face, Ronit felt his heart pound against his chest. The realization hit him hard that he was in love with her.

Ronit knew why he was here. He had thought everything through. Today, he was going to let his heart out in front of Ahaana. He wanted to know what she felt about him.

He willed to tell her that ever since he had seen her, even during the time when he hadn't as much as contacted her, he had thought about her, had missed her and that he had realised all that only when she had appeared before him again.

All that he could do was remember her face and the way her smile made his heart do something strange. He wanted to tell her everything that he felt within and then he would wait for her to reveal her feelings for him, which now he had a feeling, were mutual. Although he was a little hopeful, he still felt numbness from a fear of rejection.

Ronit wanted to do something special for her, something different. He wanted to make her happy. But before anything else, he wanted to let her know how he felt about her.

He admired the way her lustrous hair fell over her shoulders, how she shyly looked away, trying to see everything else, everything except him. The reflection of the tiny lights around them danced in her hazel eyes, making the softness underneath shiver with them. He smiled at the angelic innocence she portrayed and was about to say something when the steward arrived with a tray holding two glasses of water. He placed one before him and was about to place the other when Ronit said, "We would like mineral water please."

"Oh sure sir, I am sorry." He bent forward to take the glass back from the table when suddenly, the one that was there on his tray tumbled, spilling all over Ronit's t-shirt. Ronit got up with a jerk, startled as the sudden coolness rushed over him, making the steward step backwards, shaking with fear and regret. Ahaana was instantly at Ronit's side, holding a bunch of paper napkins from the table. She handed them to him as he grinned all of a sudden and then chuckled. Ahaana was as surprised, as the steward was relieved that Ronit was not upset.

"I... I am terribly sorry sir," he stammered.

"It is all right!" Ronit was exceptionally calm for the situation as he simply dismissed the waiter.

"Are you all right?" Ahaana hesitated as she looked at the mess he was in.

"I am fine. Don't worry. I think I'll just go and dry myself a bit," he said, pointing to the direction where the restrooms were.

Ronit smiled as he saw his reflection in the mirror while he dried himself. Some start for what he intended to say, he thought as he smirked.

"Ronit! What happened to you?" Ronit looked up astonished at the mirror and was surprised to find Soham standing right behind him. He turned around with a grin acknowledging him, "Hey buddy! What brings you here?"

Soham smiled back as he looked him up and down. "Did you just take a shower here or something?"

"The steward just spilled a glass of water over me."

"Yikes! That sounds terrible."

"It *feels* worse man," he said, mocking a shiver.

"My sympathies are with you. Need any help?"

"Nope, thanks buddy. I am all right. And this is almost dry." He pulled his t-shirt straight as he looked back up at him.

"You just got here? I was about to leave. I had stopped by for a coffee."

"Alone? Well…"

"Yes, alone! Are you here with someone?"

"Umm… yes! Just got here." Ronit hesitated for a moment, not willing to tell him about Ahaana yet, at least not until she knew what he felt.

"Great! I will make a move then."

"I'll see you out. I am heading back to my table anyway."

As they walked out, Ronit craned his neck towards the table, but Ahaana wasn't there. Looking around, he tried to search for her when all of a sudden, Soham tugged at his arm.

"What is it dude?" Ronit asked as he worried about where Ahaana had disappeared.

"Do you see that girl over there?" He was pointing at the direction of the entrance. "Look over there, dude!" Soham pressed again.

Ronit hastily turned to see where Soham was pointing and spotted Ahaana, her hands folded. He was instantly relived to find her when Soham looked at him with a big grin.

He shot him a confused glance. "You know her?"

"Know her?" He rolled his eyes. "Ronit, she is the one I have fallen for dude, the one I was going to get engaged to!"

Soham was saying something else too, but Ronit could not hear anything. He was grounded there, unable to move a muscle. *How could that be? But Ahanaa was always here, she...* he did not know how to react as he felt his palms get clammy with sweat. He kept quiet and looked back at Soham who was looking at her in a way that Ronit did not want anybody else to, except for himself. But here was Soham, telling him that even before he could let her know of his feelings for her, even before he could make her his own, he had already lost her to his childhood friend. He clenched his fists even tighter until his nails dug into his palm.

"Ronit?" Soham put a hand over his shoulders and shook him up. "Ronit?"

He jerked back to reality as he realised that he was not meant to be there in the picture at all. "Yes Soham," he gave a weak smile.

He smiled back at him and said, "So you finally get to see her now. She is the one... Ahaana! I guess you had to find out the name yourself." He grinned.

"Yes, Ahaana Agarwal!" He said nodding without any expressions.

Soham turned to look at him, surprised, "You know her? How?"

"She was the wedding planner that I had appointed!"

"Really? Wow! That is such a small world. And all this while I was trying to play 'guess the name' with you." He slapped Ronit's back fondly as he pulled him ahead. "C'mon, let us go see her. Now that you are our connecting end, I am sure I can convince her to marry me."

"Why don't you go ahead and I will follow?" Ronit offered.

"What? No way! I am not losing out on this opportunity. Just come along."

Soham almost pulled Ronit along towards where Ahaana was standing, smiling to herself, dreaming her own fantasies, unaware of what the reality was becoming altogether.

"Hi Ahaana!" Soham said cheerfully as she looked up in his direction, surprised to find him there. He moved aside and Ronit appeared from behind and stood next to him, looking away, lacking the strength to meet those eyes.

She looked at him and then back at Soham, unable to place what was happening. "What are you doing here? I mean… what's going on?"

She looked at Ronit, who finally met her gaze and managed a smile. "Ahaana, Soham is my childhood friend!"

Ahaana

"Wh… what?!" I stared at Soham and then at Ronit who was looking away, trying to hide something.

Uggh! So that was the plan? I then put the pieces together. It was all a wicked plan to convince me to accept Soham's proposal. My chest tightened as the pain of betrayal stabbed through my heart.

And here I thought, he loved me! God, it hurt!

But why play with my feelings, why pretend to like me? Did Ronit think he could woo me with his money and then break my.

Was it only an attempt to convince me into giving Soham a second chance?

I felt disgusted as the anger I felt within unfurled on my features. I knew everything now and no one could fool me. Ronit had played with my emotions.

I looked at him square in the eye. "So this is what your plan was?" I asked angrily, trying my best to control the tears that were trying hard to surface.

"What plan?" Ronit asked, unable to understand. He looked upset. *Well, he better be!*

"You thought you could convince me into marrying Soham? That's what all this was about, right?"

"What are you talking about?" Ronit said, confused.

"You know it damn well! It must have cost you a lot while you tried to convince me that you are here as a friend... taking me to fancy luncheons and dinners, only to get me to marry your friend?" I shot a disgusted look at both of them, unable to hide the pain I felt on being tricked.

"Now if you could please excuse me." I spun around angrily.

"Ahaana!" They both called in unison as I walked past them and out of the cafe. Soham stood uprooted as Ronit ran behind me. He caught up soon enough and I felt his hands on my shoulders. My heart betrayed me in spite of the anger that had welled up within, making me stop. He turned me around to face him and when I looked up into his eyes, I saw a reflection of pain. He inhaled sharply as tears ran down my face and I looked away.

"Ahaana!"

"Don't talk to me! You played with my emotions. Just because you've got power and money, don't think everybody is obliged to behave the way you want them to." I blinked back my tears, angry with myself for breaking down in front of him.

"I... I didn't mean... I am just ... sorry."

Ronit

At first, Ronit was angry that she had led him on and not mentioned anything of meeting Soham or a prospective wedding. But all that rage was replaced by agony when he saw those beautiful hazel eyes filled up with tears. His heart went out to her as he tried to take control of the ache, unable to bear the hurt that reflected on her face, in her eyes.

He forgot all about his own anger. All he wanted to do was take her into the comfort of his arms and hold her that way forever. But then, he felt a knot in his heart as he remembered that she did not belong to him at all.

"You are not sorry!" She turned around to leave again as he caught her by the arm.

"Ahaana!" He held her with all he had as he stared at her with beseeching eyes.

She struggled and let herself loose from his grasp. "Don't you dare try to touch me!" He stepped back, recoiling from her sharp words.

"You don't have a car. Please take mine," he pleaded.

"I don't need anything from you." With that, she walked faster, leaving him standing there, fighting the agony that pressed on his insides as she heard Soham shout out her name from behind.

Ahaana

I did not as much as glance behind as I hailed a cab and supplied the directions to my home. Hot tears sprang down my cheeks as I dabbed them with the napkin that I had held foolishly for Ronit when his t-shirt was soaked.

I cringed at the memory, which I couldn't believe had taken place only a few minutes ago. I was unable to believe that everything –

that look in his eyes, that effort to meet me, the words that touched my heart – all of it was only an attempt by a friend to convince me to his own benefit?

Uggh! I was better off without him. I did not have words that could describe the betrayal I felt right then. But now, what the hell was the problem with my heart.

It hurt, and hurt like never before. Saying no to Soham back there in Mumbai or refusing him a couple of days back, facing my parents, everything, was way less agonising than this one moment. And why the hell did he look at me that way? He did *not* love me, then why pretend that my words affected him.

"Why the hell am I still thinking of him? I will not! He played with me. I will get over him and forget him," I said angrily, making the taxi driver turn his head, befuddled with his passenger's behaviour.

"Sorry?" he asked.

"Nothing. Please drive!" I said as I wiped a fresh set of tears that were brimming in my eyes.

However in the world had I managed to land myself here? I heaved out a heavy sigh as the cab neared my area.

We closed in towards my house, "Here, please stop here."

I paid him and disembarked holding my bag tightly, fighting the cold air pricking my face, wet with the tears. As the cab drove out of sight, I noticed my car parked outside my house and as everything replayed in my mind all over again, I broke down right there, out in the open.

Ronit

Ronit absently walked into his room. The lights were off and he did not bother to turn them on. He crouched on the sofa near the window and closed his eyes, leaning his head back on the headrest.

He looked at the moonlight streaming through the windows of his room and then remembered those tears. The way they shined in the moonlight out there and the unbearable ache that it had caused in his chest. He knew he had hurt her, but he could not come in between them, not when he knew his friend loved her. And Ahaana, she did not even know of his feelings for her, nor had she expressed any of it herself. He couldn't fathom why she was so hurt. He knew it was the last time he saw her and the fact created a fresh prick in his heart.

He did not mention anything to Soham and knew that he would take care of her. With him out of the picture, Soham would eventually try and make her his. The thought made him cringe as he felt his jaws tremble. He brought a hand towards his cheeks as he touched the wetness, surprised at the fact that he was crying.

He had to move on, he decided, he had to move away, right then, so that he did not come in anybody's way.

FOUR MONTHS LATER

Ahaana

I was busy making a note of the requirement by the caterers when Ansh came by at my desk. "I have booked the tickets for tomorrow. The flight is at noon. We all will leave for the airport at ten in the morning?"

"Fine! I will keep that in mind. Thanks," I said, not looking up, but still writing in my little journal.

"Ahaana! It is high time you let go of the past," he said placing a hand on my shoulder.

"What past?" I didn't look up as I said that.

"You know what I am talking about." He shut my journal, pushing it aside and sat on the table.

"What?" I looked up at him, irritated.

"Ahaana, you have a wedding to attend!"

I ignored his words as I opened my journal once again.

"C'mon Ahaana!"

"Stop it Ansh. I am fine. Why don't you just let me be? I know I cannot sulk for long and I will not."

"It is Rahul's wedding! At least use that as an excuse to get over what happened.

"Ansh, I have moved on."

"Yes, I can see that."

I heaved a sigh at my friend's outburst, trying to get rid of the agony I still felt within. "You know what, I fail to understand why the instant I say that I am happy, the same second my life plans otherwise."

He could probably see the dejection in the tears I tried to hide as he impatiently exhaled, seeming frustrated even further.

"Ahaana… to hell with everything, just get that stupid smile of yours back, will you?" he said with an agitated fervour.

I smiled in spite of myself at his words as he put his arms around me, pulling me towards him in one of the most needed hugs.

"Good progress," he said, smiling fondly down at me.

As he let go and walked back towards his table, I sadly noticed my reflection on the dark screen of the computer. The stark feeling of betrayal was vivid even now. I could still remember the pain I had felt and even now my heart ached for Ronit.

But Ansh was right. I had to move on. Ronit had never loved me and I had never got a chance to let him know of my feelings for him. And after that incident, I did not have to. It was evident that everything that he had done was only for his childhood friend Soham. Ronit had not contacted me after that night. Although it was what I had needed, it hurt as it confirmed all the doubts I had. And Soham, I had denied keeping any sort of contact with him. They had both moved on and here I was, were surviving only on those memories.

Yes, I had to move on. It was time to be a part of someone else's happiness all over again, only this time, I was happy for that someone as well.

Confirming my thoughts to myself, I looked up to find Ansh and Mishka engaged in a deep conversation, Mishka sheepishly grinning at stances and blushing involuntarily at some. I sighed, thinking this was another blunder that was happening here, unless Mishka confronted Ansh about how she felt about him. I did not want her to land the way I did. It was unbearably painful. And Mishka had a crush on this guy since practically ages.

Another mission, I found myself thinking as I walked over to them. Before I reached them, Ansh was already on his way back towards his desk. *Good,* I thought.

I walked past him, giving him a smile, over to where Mishka sat. Seeing me approach, she nodded with a wide smile.

It must have been a task to deal with me sulking all the time all these four months, I thought guiltily as I tried to reflect the same grin on my face.

"Hi Ahaana!" Mishka said brightly, making me feel better about what I thought and was about to say.

"Hey Mishka! Got a minute to spare?"

"Yes sure. Why don't you sit?"

"Nope. Let's go take a walk?"

"Right now?"

"Yes, it's lovely outside today."

"Okay," she put her laptop on hibernation and shut the screen as she stepped out from behind her desk and stood beside me.

As we walked out, I sneaked a look at Ansh who was eyeing us curiously. When our eyes met, he arched his eyebrows as if to ask where we were heading. I simply nodded towards the entrance.

As we walked out, I headed toward the garden chairs we had set up last week, making it our own personal space for relaxation at work.

"What happened?" she asked me as we sat down, a worried expression taking charge.

I cleared my throat as if searching for the right words.

"Is something wrong Ahaana? Are you all right?" she asked.

"I am fine, I am fine! It is just that there is something that I want to discuss with you," I paused and sighed and added, "or rather something that I want to ask you."

"Me? Oh, what is it?" She looked worried.

"Mish…. You are in love with Ansh, right?" I asked her directly, looking at her. She looked away immediately.

"Have you lost it? N-noo… there is no such thing. I mean Ansh is so… definitely sweet. I mean he is so handsome and he is so nice and everything in between… uhh… but I mean, I like him, but I don't *love* him Ahaana!" She fumbled with words as she looked away and then back at me and then at her feet.

I smiled as she fidgeted and looked everywhere else, but at me. Placing a hand on her shoulder, I said, "Mish, I know exactly how you feel about him. From the start, when you used to think that we both were going around until when you became close to us and realised that we were both just best friends. I have seen it in your eyes and I know you love him. Just be frank and tell me."

"A… Ahaana!" she stammered. "B-but…"

"Admit it Mish, if you love him, let him know, because if you lose him, you won't be able to forgive yourself for not even trying. You are just too shy and if you keep your emotions hidden, you just might end up hurting yourself."

Mishka looked up at me then, suddenly feeling at a loss of words. "Ahaana, but I don't think Ansh will ever like me."

"How could you possibly know?"

She looked down and then said, "But I don't think I can tell him. I don't *know* how to tell him."

"You love him, right?" I asked looking up directly to gather a glimpse of her confidence.

"Yes!" Mishka replied sheepishly.

"And you wouldn't want to lose him, would you?"

"Do you think he could be mine?" She looked towards me with hopeful eyes.

"Of course he can! All you have to do is go and tell him. Let him know, Mish!" I smiled brightly as I revelled in the fact that Mishka understood her priorities and would do something about it.

"Okay. But I am scared."

"I will help you with that."

I knew exactly what I would do as I winked at her and told her what I had planned, whispering into her ears, just in case! Mishka grinned back nervously as she began to believe in my master plan.

"But how will you do that?"

"Oh, you leave that one to me!" I smiled broadly as I happily delved into what I was planning, finally feeling a little spark ignite within me.

While we both walked inside, Mishka kept her eyes down as she went to her desk while I walked back towards my own, both of us ignoring Ansh even though he was curiously eyeing our way, unsure of what we were up to.

I dialled the number of my travel agent and opened the email that Ansh had just sent me of our tickets for tomorrow's flight to Delhi.

"Hi Mr Srikant, Ahaana here. I wanted you to please postpone my flight tickets to the evening flight."

"Yes, Ansh and Mishka will travel by the same flight. I have an urgent meeting that I must attend, thus I will have to cancel my afternoon flight and need one in the evening." After listening to the confirmation at the other end, I supplied, "Okay. Thank you so much," and with that I hung up, grinning broadly, giving a mental pat on my back. Glancing in Mishka's direction, I gave her a wink to which she giggled like a schoolgirl.

Ronit

Ronit kept himself busy throughout the days and made sure that he was tired enough so that the minute he got into his bed, he would fall asleep. But yet, in spite of all the efforts that he would put in, sleep was scarce. It had been more than four months and yet, all he could remember was Ahaana and the way those tears broke his heart, over and over again. The very next day he had flown out from Bangalore, to head the Delhi office.

He had not spoken to Soham since then and he did not have the nerve to face him yet. He assumed that he must have convinced Ahanaa and by now they would have been engaged as well. He recoiled at the thought and felt guilty at the same time.

He was sitting in his conference room, looking at all the empty chairs before him. Exhausted, with this being the third consecutive meeting of the day, he put his head back, trying to fight the increasing headache. Suddenly his telephone beeped, making him jerk at the sudden intervention. He pressed the button on the speaker as the voice of his secretary filled the silent room with sudden reverberation.

"Sir, Mr Soham is here to see you."

Ronit grimaced at the name, unable to fathom the coincidence. What was Soham doing in Delhi, he thought to himself when the voice of his secretary broke in the silence again.

"What must I tell him sir?"

"Please send him in," he said politely as he sat up straight, bracing himself to face a million questions.

He waited as Soham entered, standing up to greet him with a hug.

"Hey buddy! Where have you been?" Soham said brightly as he hugged him back.

"Am here, it is you who has been lost." He tried to sound as normal as he could.

"How are you and Ahaana doing?" he asked naively.

"Me and Ahaana?" Soham looked at him with a puzzled expression as he took his seat opposite Ronit's chair.

"Yeah? How is she?"

"She must be fine!" He answered casually.

"What do you mean she must be? You guys are together, right?" Ronit looked at him confused.

Soham smirked as he looked away.

"What?" Ronit was nearing the limit to his patience as he waited for Soham to say something.

"We are not together Ronit. We never were. That night, at the coffee shop, was the last time I saw her. I tried contacting her after that, but she refused to see me and then I went back to Mumbai."

"You both are not together?" Ronit felt a thud in his heart as he grasped the information. Something snapped within as he sat back on his chair with a sudden jerk. Soham immediately sprang onto his feet to grab hold of him, unable to understand why Ronit behaved that way.

"No, we are not. Are you okay dude?" He looked concerned.

"I am fine." Ronit looked straight ahead, not able to think about anything, anyone but her, not able to see anything but those saddened eyes, he could hear nothing but that silent cry. "Soham, I've got to be somewhere. Can I see you later?"

"Sure! Is everything okay?"

"Yes it is. I will see you later. Sorry." With that, he shot up from his chair and within minutes, grabbed his blazer and his cell phone and dashed out of his cabin.

On his way out, he looked at his secretary who sprang out of her chair as she saw him approach her suddenly. "Book me a seat on the next flight to Bangalore," he commanded and she immediately followed his instructions.

He sprinted towards the exit and sat inside his car as swiftly as possible and gave directions for the airport. He had been hit hard with the fact that Soham had laid before him. He felt happy and worried, both at the same time. He had to see her, to tell her that he loved her, more than anything else, more than anyone else.

He did not know where Ahaana would be, if she were seeing anyone by now, or worse, if she was married. But he had to try, this one last time, for the sake of his sanity. He took out his cell phone and dialled her number.

He waited impatiently as the call got connected and sighed loudly as it went unreachable. Nervous and not having faith in his fate, he asked his driver to hurry. It was two in the afternoon and the flight to Bangalore was at four. He could still reach her on time. He would find her. He was determined to do so.

Love is what Ronit felt at that moment. It was *love* that ran in his veins, making him feel more alive than he had ever been in ages. He did not know what awaited him, but he was certain that he had to try. He had to know where Ahaana was and how she felt about him. He wanted to tell her that he loved her, that he had always loved her, but it was only time that had kept them apart.

He wanted to tell her that he had taken her out that night to tell her how he felt about her and not anything else that circumstances had led her to believe. He felt disgusted at the thought itself and fought back angry tears as his car screeched to a halt in front of the airport.

Ronit rushed in. He would reach Bangalore by half past six. He calculated the time until he could meet her and grew impatient with every passing minute. There was an adrenaline rush within him that made him feel like he had her, and yet he might lose her forever.

Ahaana

Smiling inwardly, I relished the fact that I had successfully sent Mishka and Ansh together on the flight to Delhi. Mishka would have enough time to let Ansh know how she felt about him and at the end of the day, when I would meet them, I would have happiness all around me. I was excited about what lay ahead.

Having brought my bags to the office, I decided to complete some pending work before I left for the airport. I checked my wrist watch and realised that it was already five. My flight was at eight. I called for Joshi and gave him all the required instructions.

"Three days Joshi, you will have to make sure everything goes on smoothly. You can call us on our cell phones at any time if there is any problem. All right?"

"Ji madam ji, you don't worry. We will take care," he replied confidently, making me grin.

"And make sure you give the office keys at my house or Krish bhaiya will come and pick it up."

"Ji madam ji." He nodded again, smiling, making me smile back, thinking about the fun that lay ahead.

After a quick nod, I picked up my purse and walked out. I was in no hurry since the ride to the airport was only twenty minutes from our office.

Minutes later, I hopped into a cab. I couldn't help thinking about how Mishka must've told Ansh about her feelings and smiled in spite of myself. There was something about love that kept me going, though I had had some terrible experience with the emotion myself.

The thought threw me back onto the memories of Ronit, but soon got overshadowed by his betrayal as I immediately decided for the umpteenth time that it was not love that we had shared. Trying to get his thoughts out of my head, I took out my cell phone. I was surprised to find it switched off.

When did I turn it off, I thought to myself. Suddenly the driver was pulling the car into the driveway of the airport. Keeping my phone back inside my purse, I disembarked. I walked to get myself a trolley while the driver placed my luggage upon it. Thanking him, I paid and walked inside slowly, still having plenty of time at my disposal.

Ronit

Ronit reached Bangalore airport by six thirty. He was glad that his flight was on time. Having no luggage that he had checked in earlier, he directly hailed a cab and gave instructions towards Ahaana's workplace. Even the twenty-minute drive seemed like eternity as he waited impatiently for his destination. He kept replaying the events of his last meet with Ahaana, over and over again, feeling all those emotions rush back like it had all happened yesterday.

The driver pulled in front of her office as he hurriedly took out some cash, paid him and stepped out, feeling the blood rush insanely through his veins. Not waiting for the change, he slowly walked inside, preparing himself for a glimpse of that one face, which had stolen the peace of his mind.

He walked in, fixing his eyes onto the desk, which he knew belonged to her. But he found the desk empty. He searched at either sides and found the other two desks of her friends empty as well. Unsure of what to make of it, he searched for someone who could answer him, when a man with glasses and a box in his hand, approached him.

"May I help you sir?" he asked.

"Hi… yes please! I was looking for Ahaana?"

"Oh! Madam ji has gone out of town sir! You are?"

"Out of town? Where? When did she leave?"

"Do you know her sir?"

"Yes, I am her friend, Ronit Malhotra. Could you please tell me where she has gone?"

"She just left today, sir ji, one hour back. She is going to Dilli. She will be back after three days."

"Oh okay. Thank you so much." He gave a quick glance at his watch. He did not have time to get worked up over how fate was playing games with him.

It was 7 and he knew the next flight to Delhi would be at 8. He knew he would find her at the airport. He turned to rush out as the man called behind him, "Sir ji, I will tell her you came."

"That won't be needed, thank you," he called out as he rushed on his way outside. He realised then that he had no mode of transport and he had foolishly left the cab. Angry at not thinking about it ahead of time, he rushed back in.

"Excuse me?" he called out loudly.

The man came out quickly, reciprocating to the urgency in his voice.

"I don't have my car; do you have any vehicle that I can borrow? I really need to go to the airport urgently."

"Sir ji, I have my bike." He looked Ronit up and down, as if figuring whether he was worth taking the risk. Convinced, he offered, "You can have it sir ji.

"Thank you." Ronit held him tightly by the shoulders, thanking his stars and the man in front. "May I have the keys please?"

"Ye... yes sir," he hesitated before handing over the keys, but finally gave them over to him.

"Thank you, Mr....?"

"Joshi, I am Joshi, sir ji."

"Thank you so much Mr Joshi. I am Ronit Malhotra and I will be indebted to you forever!"

He smiled and shied away in response as Ronit took the keys and rushed out.

He hopped onto the bike. As he keyed in the ignition, his hands froze and his chest felt heavy. He recalled the accident his brother had had and instantly felt paralysed. Shaking his head, he took a deep breath and brought the bike to life. Feeling a lump in his throat, he settled and then as if suddenly in control, he sped towards where Ahaana was.

They had just been served their meals on the flight and this was one of Ansh's favourite parts of travelling by air. While most of the airways now had terminated this ritual and went on delivering café takeaways, he made sure he purchased a meal before booking his flights. Though it sounded childish, he had nothing to shy away from. He grinned as he took out the cutlery from its cover and opened the small container carrying the butter. He sliced the bun and spread some of it generously, as if it were the most delicious thing he had ever eaten; and then he indulged into it. Mishka, who had been behaving absurdly since the last hour, saw that sight and burst out laughing.

"It seems like you are feasting at some fine dining restaurant," she commented in between giggles.

"Oh, you bet! It is no less than any, trust me Mish!" he said grinning back.

The way he said Mish made her blush and she looked away. She knew that in the next hour, their flight would land and then she would never get a chance as good as this to tell him how she felt about him. And if she did not now, Ahaana would practically kill her.

"Umm... ahem!" She cleared her throat as Ansh looked at her with a questioning glance. She hesitated, fiddling with her fork. "Ansh, I... I uh, I need to tell you something," she finally managed.

"Sure, tell me? Is it something to do with our new project?" he said with his mouth full.

"Huh? No... no! It is not that. It is actually something else."

"Okay?" He looked at her and waited and when no reply came, he stressed, "What is it Mish? Any problem?"

"No Ansh, no problem! Nothing, I was just thinking about something, but it's not too important."

"Are you sure?" He looked at her, confused.

"Yes, yes! I am sure," she sighed. As she thought to herself, she realised that she would not be able to live without this person who was sitting right next to her. She suddenly felt guilty, as if she was letting herself down. As she debated within herself, but did not notice that Ansh was eying her carefully, understanding the fact that something was definitely going on in her head.

"Okay Mish, out with it! Something is definitely bothering you," he said concerned.

She looked away, now on the verge of fighting back her tears. She had never been this helpless before. She looked at him, hoping that he would somehow understand what her heart wanted to let him know.

It was then that Ansh realised that she was almost about to cry. A little shiver ran down his spine. He looked up at her.

"Hey Mishka, what happened?" Ansh put a hand upon hers as he felt her fingers tighten into a fist underneath his palm.

"Ansh, I don't know how to say it... it will sound so crazy."

"Tell me, I am sure it will be all right if you let out whatever is troubling you." He felt something pound against his chest as he discerned the fact that her sad eyes caused something absurd within him.

"Ansh, I..." she paused again and this time deciding to simply let go, she said the words, "I have fallen in love with you."

As she said those words, she could not muster up the courage to look up into his eyes. She held her fist a little more tightly, prepared for the withdrawal of his hand from above hers. But instead, he let them be in place. She nervously managed to look up, prepared to meet the resentful look in his eyes, but instead, what she faced was compassion and understanding.

"Ansh," before she could say anything else, he silenced her.

"Mishka, I... I..."

"No Ansh, it is really okay. I mean, you don't have to like me back, I just..." She stifled a small giggle, trying to hide her feelings as she continued, "I just wanted to let it out."

Ansh simply looked on, unable to believe that the love he had been looking for was in front of him all this while and all he had to do was simply look with his heart and eyes wide open. He could understand now why it affected him the way it did, to see pain in her eyes. Without saying another word, he lifted her hand and held it firmly, close to his heart.

He wanted to remove any doubts that she might have in her mind and wanted her to know that he had accepted her already. Mishka had always been a shy person and it must have taken a lot of effort on her part to vent out her emotions. As he held onto her hands, she looked up at him, expectantly.

"Mish, I think you have said enough!" he said, mocking indifference. For what he was known for, Ansh had to lighten the air between them and as he said that, he dropped her hands, making her recoil with the fear of rejection.

"I... I am sorry," she stammered as she looked down and then towards the aisle of the flight. She was conscious that the other passengers might notice her failure and clasped her hands tightly.

Ansh grinned mischievously and then leaned in closer to her. He whispered into her ears, "So, if this is the case, then I don't think you would..." he paused as she stammered, "No... no, I won't quit work."

He grinned to himself again and then after clearing his throat he said in the same soft tone, a low whisper, "Good! But what I was saying is, with your feelings and all that, I guess you would *not* mind getting married to me, would you?" He grinned as he said that, as an astonished Mishka looked on, nervousness giving away to wonderment. Her mouth was left ajar, her eyes searching his for any sign of irony, as she unbelievingly stared back at him.

"*What?*" she shrieked, unable to fathom the words that she had just heard.

"Yeah!" He simply put his hand back over hers, squeezing it tightly. Her heartbeat oscillated, making her shiver in delight.

"Yeah!" she echoed his tone as he gave a soft laugh, thanking her heavens and Ahaana, who was out there waiting for the other flight. Her day was made as she leaned into him, inhaling in his scent and basking in the satisfaction of his protective arms around her.

Ronit

Ahaana was lost in the world of the book that she was reading as she waited for the announcement of her flight, unaware that Ronit was engaged in the pursuit of finding her. He had reached the airport and it was already going to be half past seven. He knew though that he still had ample time for Ahaana's flight to be announced and was confident that he would find her. But he still did not know why his heartbeat kept doing the irritable somersaults inside his chest.

He believed with all his heart that what he felt for Ahaana was pure and real. He knew she might still be angry with him, but he also believed that he had a place within her heart. Even if they hadn't confessed it, he had seen it in her eyes four months ago.

He parked Joshi's bike carefully, ensuring he did not mess up things in haste and went towards the departure area. For once, he was glad about his power and grateful for his rich profile for he knew a lot of authorities at the airport that could help him get inside the departure area.

He sought help from the manager on duty and after convincing him that he would be back soon, that he had to meet someone very important, he got his way into the lobby where the passengers awaited the arrival of their flights.

As he entered, he scanned the area for that one face that had taken his breath away and had given him long sleepless nights.

He spotted her, seated all by herself, near the window, engrossed into something he could not see, her back towards him. Her soft hair caressed her shoulders, a loose strand flowing over one side of her face, troubling her eyes, which she kept tucking back in behind her ear. He stood there, unable to muster up enough strength to bridge the gap of the last few steps between them.

Ahaana

I shut the book that I had been reading, running a finger over the embossed design on the cover. After a long, long time, I felt a little better. But now, suddenly as I acknowledged the fact, that feeling of hurt crept back in, making me shift uncomfortably.

I looked outside the huge glass window and noticed the darkness outside. A reflection of the people sitting in the waiting area was all that I could see on the glass.

Memories of Ronit were trying to invade my peace of mind all over again and I was trying hard to push them aside. Deciding to divert myself from my thoughts, I took out my cell phone. As I looked onto the blank dark screen I sighed, realising that I had forgotten to switch on my phone since the last time I had seen it off. Turning it on, I waited for the screen to brighten up. *No wonder I haven't got any calls as yet,* I thought to myself. I dialled the number to my office to find out if they had closed it yet or not. It went on a no reply and I smiled satisfied that Joshi had closed things on time. I decided to keep my phone back inside the pocket of my jeans, when at the same instant it started vibrating again. Exhaling softly, I answered it without looking at who the caller was, knowing it was Mom.

"Hey Ma!" I said without waiting for her to begin. "I am sorry, I did not realise that my phone was switched off, so please don't get angry, okay?"

There was no answer at the other end and that made me raise my eyebrows as I contemplated mistaken identity.

"Hello??" I said again and was about to see the screen for who the caller was when a familiar male voice spoke from the other end.

"Hello Ahaana!"

I felt my heart stop as I placed the voice of the caller. But still not believing my heart or my ears, I asked again, "Who is this?"

"Ronit," he said softly, making me cringe at the confirmation of my fears. Painful agony swept through me as I heard the voice that I did not realise I was craving to hear. The agonizing desire gave way to the pent up anger that I had suppressed all this while.

Why was he calling me now, I thought angrily, as I fought the tears pricking behind my eyes, at the same time unable to ignore the happiness that I felt within.

"Why are you calling me?" I spoke my thoughts aloud, reeling in the depth of the games my emotions were playing within me. I felt anger and all the pain creep back in, making me shiver with the intensity of the agony I felt upon listening to that voice again.

He did not respond instantly and then, after what felt like an eternity, he answered, "Will it be too much to ask if I said I just want you to turn around?"

"Huh? I don't understand wh…" I spun around, only to find him standing right behind, holding his cell phone by his ears, wearing a smile and something like, I could not point it out, but *longing* hidden in his gorgeous brown eyes. I felt my breath choke in my throat as I sprang onto my feet. Realising that I was still holding my phone by my ears, I dropped my hands down by my side.

His hair was flying in all directions, like he had just been out from a marathon. Small sweat beads covered his forehead and his breathing was heavy and fast. A tremor shook me at the effect he still had on me. I tried to say something in response, but words seemed to be stuck in my throat. A mixture of pain and happiness invaded my soul, making me want to turn and run away from him right then. Yet, I found myself grounded in front of him. All my reserves were trying to protect me from the stinging of tears in my eyes, as I stared at him unbelievably.

"Ronit?" I whispered, confusion taking over my fears, unable to recognise the sound of my own voice.

"Ahaana," he said as he stepped a little closer. I instantly backed out and unknowingly stepped upon the pedestal of the set of chairs. I was about to trip when his firm hands grasped me at the small of my back, steadying me as he held on to me. A wild shot of current darted through my veins at the spot where our skin met and I immediately let go of his hand.

I stared at him through the tears that had involuntarily sprung into my eyes, pricking and blurring out his face.

Ronit

Ronit recoiled at the sight of her tears, remembering the last time he had seen them. In spite of her refusal, he brought his hand towards her face, wiping away the saline drops that had now flowed over to her cheeks, with his thumb. It tore his insides to see her tremble that way and made him want to simply lay his protective arms around her, holding her into him forever.

"No Ahaana. Please don't cry," he said softly as she stayed still in front of him, her head bent down. She did not say a word in response. He felt invisible to the crowd near the waiting lounge as his eyes focused upon the only face that had conquered his heart since the first time he had seen it. A renewed surge of emotions took over him as he fought back his own tears, realizing that he could not imagine a life without her now!

"Ahaana! I am sorry. I am so sorry about everything." He was suddenly desperate to have her. Pleading his heart out, he yearned for her to let go of the past and come into his waiting arms.

"What for Ronit? It is all past now. I do not understand what has brought you here," she coughed up, trying to control the salty stream from breaking down the walls that she had created within her heart.

Seeing her fight back increased his agony.

"Ahaana, please. You have to listen to me," he pleaded, not letting go of her arm.

"Why?"

"The other day..." he began in spite of her refusal to hear him out, "the last time when I met you, at the coffee shop, I was not there trying to convince you about Soham."

She looked at him scornfully, not believing his words. "Yeah? Then what was he doing there with you?"

"I did not even know that it was *you* who Soham was going to get engaged to and that it was *you* for whom he had fallen," he said in one breath, making her jerk back. "I know you don't believe me right now, but please do. It was as much of a surprise for me, as it was for you. I had also found out that same time that the girl he was after was you, Ahaana. And I knew he was in love with you and I just thought it would be better if I moved out of the picture."

A fresh stream of tears ran down her face, making Ronit ache harder.

"Then why have you come back?" she asked.

"Because.....*I* am in love with you," he said softly, staring at her, deep in the eyes, pain overpowering his calm.

She shook her head in disapproval of what he was saying, not believing a word, although he begged for her heart to accept it.

"Why did you not tell me then?" she cried.

"I did not know whether you liked me back or not, and if you did not, then I thought it would be better to sacrifice my love for you when I knew my best friend was deeply in love with you as well."

"How nice, Mr Malhotra, and this is definitely the right way to treat the person you love. Just decide for her who she must fall in love with. And then, if you *have* decided that, then *why have you come back*? Is it to question why I denied Soham?" she choked again, making it unable to bear the pain, like a fire burning within his heart. She met his gaze again, "Well? If that is your question, then I refused him because I loved you back. I loved you even before I knew it was happening to me. And you, you just walked out on me."

Her words ripped him on the inside. He held her by her arm, bent down to take her luggage and pulled her along to the lounge nearby. He did not want her to be a shattered, fragile sight, not for anybody. She obeyed him then and tugged along with him to a quiet place inside the lounge. She looked frail and torn and Ronit could only look away to refrain from grasping her into his arms right then.

"I know I was foolish, I know I should have asked you, but now Ahaana, I know I love you and that you love me back." He held her face in his hands as he felt tears fill his eyes. "What I want is for you to know that I am not going to let go of you. Not now, not ever – never again. I don't care what happened in the past and I don't care what went wrong and why. I simply know that you belong to me, and that right here, I will make you believe that I love you." He held her hand towards his heart and closed his fist around it. He stepped closer, leaning down towards her face and looked at her into the eyes as she fought back a fresh set of tears. And then, he cupped her face in his hands, "Ahaana, I love you from within my soul and promise to keep you in my arms for the rest of my life. I swear that these are the last tears that you shed because of me."

He wiped them with his thumb, as she broke down into uncontrollable sobs.

"Please, make me yours?" he pleaded as he felt his vision of her get blurred because of his own tears. She let herself fall into his arms as he wrapped them tightly around her, and they both broke down, letting the one emotion they both lived, overwhelming them, defining their identity.

Ahaana whispered back, softly, unable to bear the tide of happiness that swelled in her chest, "I love you too Ronit. I have always loved you." She cried, as he nodded into her hair and stroked her back. She looked up at him then and he smiled back at her. She stood on her toes as he bent forward and slowly touched his lips with hers. They shared their first and the most passionate kiss, sealing them into a bond that would last until eternity.

Holding his head back, Ronit smiled into the eyes of the girl he loved madly, "I love you madly, soon to be Mrs Ahaana Malhotra!"

Naughtiness sprang into Ahaana's eyes as she responded with a grin, "Who said anything about marriage?"

"You wouldn't?" Hurt spread back into his eyes, making her heart rip as she held him back, tighter this time.

"I was just kidding," she said softly.

"I know, soon to be Mrs Ahaana Ronit Malthora," he said possessively as he winked, making her stare at him unbelievingly. As she mocked hitting a closed fist over his chest, they both indulged into fits of a laughter that promised them a future they had always yearned for.

They held onto each other then, feeling their heartbeats echo in the silence of the lounge area. They stood, oblivious to the world around them, whispering promises of love, binding two souls forever.

Epilogue

"The heart has its own language, which only the eyes can fathom... The eyes - that are the windows to the soul."

That marked the beginning of a reconciliation which was destined to become so much more. Two lives, two souls, entwined together to give a new meaning to love, to life. Ronit and Ahaana wore their wedding rings soon after they attended Rahul's wedding and then went together to bless their best friends, Ansh and Mishka on theirs, all throughout spreading the message of love, faith and belief. In those small gemstones, the colour white that adorned both their fingers, was the story of their romance, their passion and their love, that grew with every passing second. And with it, came the promise to live for each other, to sleep and to wake up, looking into each other's eyes, in one another's arms.

No matter what the human mind can create, the heart designs an entirely different melody, where two souls, even though situated at two different parts of the world, find a way to make their hearts beat together.

With that, is it any wonder that god, the invisible hand, would make a young man commit his soul to another of his creation – the woman – binding the two souls together, making them one equal, an entire entity, a symbol of love – just like Ronit and Ahaana?